BREAK THIS HOUSE

BREA

T

HO

BREAK THIS HOUSE

CANDICE ILOH

DUTTON BOOKS

DUTTON BOOKS

An imprint of Penguin Random House LLC, New York

First published in the United States of America by Dutton Books,
an imprint of Penguin Random House LLC, 2022

Visit us online at penguinrandomhouse.com.

Library of Congress Cataloging-in-Publication Data is available.

Book manufactured in Canada

ISBN 9780525556237

10 9 8 7 6 5 4 3 2 1

FRI
Design by Anna Booth
Text set in Feijoa

For Mom

Dear Reader,

A lot of us are taught that if a feeling is too ugly or too loud, we should make sure we hide it. That there are things we shouldn't admit to, because what would they say about us? What would it say about us if we are angry at someone we love? If we cursed something or someone we are supposed to fear or respect, what kind of person would that make us? We are told a lot of things about how we should feel or behave when something bad happens. When the unexpected suddenly changes our lives, there seem to be all these rules about how to deal with it. But here's the thing: No one even knows what they're talking about. Not really. At least not about you. We all deal with it all differently.

The truth is I wrote this book to say the things I'm not supposed to say. I wanted to tell a story where the person in pain doesn't pretend. And I wanted to explore what it looks like to feel all these things at the same time: joy, love, rage. All of it.

I say all this to say, this book is going to get super real. And a little reckless. As you read it, some hard things may come up. You might experience some intense feelings. Particularly about **death and existence**. You'll probably laugh at some strange things too. But because I don't know you personally, I can't tell you what you can or can't handle. Only you can do that. I'm just here to say, take good care of yourself, friend. And whenever you need it, take breaks.

Thanks for being here. You're in for a wild ride.

With love,
Candice

Promise that you will

           sing

              about me.

                    KENDRICK LAMAR

PROLOGUE

A rumor about Obsidian, Michigan, goes like this:

There once were two girls who broke things. But not in the way that anyone might think. The girls didn't break regular things like glass or nails or bones. The girls broke bigger things—things they said could never work for them in the first place. At least not after everything that happened. Not after so much changed. At first, they broke promises they'd made to each other. Next, it was their bond. Then, it was the belief that anything could last forever or come back. Because look at us, they thought. Look at this family. Look at this place. The girls grew so used to things being broken that trying to fix them became the greatest chaos of all.

At first.

BREA

ONE

"Aye, Pop. you stink."

"Hello to you, too, Minah," Pop says, cutting me off with an eye roll right before mushing a kiss into my forehead. I catch a whiff of stale cow blood before he continues past me into the kitchen. "Relax— I'm on my way to the shower already. Ain't gotta say that shit to me every day. Can't expect your pop to quit his job just 'cause you protesting dead animals now."

Everything about me that Pop and I disagree on he calls a "protest." Us "new-grade young people"—as he labels us—always gotta be hollerin' about something that worked just fine back when he was a teenager, and the problem with us is that we got too many feelings about things that are simple, like food and the moon. According to Pop, we spend too much time fussing over everybody needing to be vegetarians when what we need to be doing is training our ears to be able to hear real music again.

"First of all, the shower's that way. That's the fridge, just in case you got a little confused. Second, ain't nobody protesting. Just think they prolly should have showers in that death chamber you workin' at, bro." I don't understand how a person can live with themselves after spending they whole day slaughtering everything that bleeds and then selling it to somebody on a foam plate and wrapped in plastic to take home to they families. I mean, it used to be nearly impossible for me to walk past Shake Shack without gettin' got just last summer, but still. I've been delivered from my ignorance.

"All right, tell me something, *bro*," he says, pulling off his pit-stained white tee, now turned a dingy yellow. "How could a place that pays for *all of this*," he says, pausing to look around the house like it's the second coming of the Trump Towers, "be a *death chamber?*" He waits for the gulp of beer to slosh down his throat before flashing his "gotcha" smile. He wouldn't be himself if he didn't pause for dramatic effect when he's tryna prove that he's right.

"Now, you know 'all of this' don't mean nothin' in Crown Heights. We live in a box, Pop. And I'm pretty sure killing all god's animal children every day and calling yourself a butcher classifies it as peak chamber of deaths. Like, by definition." A vision of the Trump Towers flashes before my eyes in my imaginary Google search for American Chamber of Deaths before I shake it away to finish closing the deal. "But I'll say a special prayer for your soul if I can get ten bucks."

"You ain't no real vegan," he says, tossing me a sweaty, crumpled twenty from his jeans pocket. "I'll believe that holistic mess you into now when you stop taking all my damn money. Shouldn't your no-waste lifestyle be costing me less . . . or something like that? Get me two gallons of water and a bag of them plantain chips. The garlic kind." Pop always gives me more than I ask for with a side of fake complaints. He puts on this act every time I ask for a little change to go to the store, but he's always telling me that this is what he's here for. And he's always been here.

"Damn, Pop. Wasn't tryna do all that. I was just tryna get something to drink."

"'Damn, Pop!'" His over-the-top impressions of me be having me weak. It doesn't matter that my voice is almost as deep as his or that raising me ain't like raising those other girls I go to school with. I always sound like a spoiled, whiny-ass chick who hangs out at the mall all day with Daddy's credit card when Pop spits back the things I say at me. Full-on squeak mode.

"Firstly, watch your mouth. Nothing's free, Minah. Plus, what you need a whole ten dollars for when you know all you 'bout to get is some orange juice and coconut water? Fancy-ass bodega-snacks tax?" he says, scrunching up his face in disgust at the latter. "You're welcome." He finally turns his back down the hall toward the bathroom.

"Breath gon' be funkier than the homeless man on the train," I mumble under my breath, pulling on a sneaker.

"What you say?!" he screams over the running bathwater as I pull on the other. I must got the youngest dad in the whole hood. He hears everything. The giant mirror leaned up against the wall just inside our front door gives me a chance to glance over my look. I reach for my biggest pair of sunglasses and pull a bucket hat low over my twists. A decent bodega-run disguise. I tug a little at each corner of my T-shirt and check out my ass in my favorite jeans. Loose enough.

"Nothing . . . nothing. I'ma be back."

———

Our side of Crown Heights almost feels like don't nobody go to work around here. Cars speed up and down the street like it ain't kids around to worry about. Buses push off the stop even though they see somebody runnin' to catch it. Dollar cabs blast horns loud enough you probably could hear them all the way in Bed-Stuy. Gossipy Trini grandmothers take their sweet time, clogging up the sidewalk in front of the West Indian market, squeezing mangoes and avocados checking to see if they're ready to eat. And all of them scoot slow and unbothered

with no signs of whether all the noise gets on their nerves. Each wrinkled hand remains steady despite how soca blasts from cars driving by
behind them, shaking the whole block's concrete.

"Yoooooo, mamaaaaaa. You got some extra change? Can you get
me a soda?" I thought walking fast behind my biggest, blackest sunglasses, thumbing my phone like I got business, would have sent some
type of signal to Old Man that I wasn't tryna do all that today. He
pauses, smiles with all his grayish ancient teeth, hands stuffed into his
pockets. The no-need-to-be-scared-of-me stance I'm used to seeing on
him, carefully chosen in hopes that I'll let my guard down.

"You want a coffee?" I offer instead, continuing to walk. I don't
ever buy him soda. Or any of those other fake chemical excuses for
food they got in there. Water, coffee, and sandwiches prepared on the
grill only when I got it like that.

"I'll take a coffee," he accepts. The door jingles as I push quickly
into the corner bodega. Old Man trails, head lowered, behind me. He
makes a beeline for the coffee station while I split off down the aisle
with all the chips. Fur grazes my ankle, and my instinct is to jump, but
I fall back at ease looking down to see Bodega Cat greet me the way
she always does. I try my best not to think about where she's been or
what she's been doing with her life. Cats can't take off their shoes after
coming in from New York City streets like Pop makes me do, a never-
ending reminder of how dirty this city is. And I don't care that cats
clean themselves all day with their own saliva. You can't convince me
licking yourself makes you clean. I grab Pop's funky garlic chips—the
purple bag with the palm tree next to the bright green lettering—right
before heading to the back coolers for my juice and coconut water. Pop
thinks he knows me or something. And how he gon' send me in here

for two whole jugs of water? Don't none of these bodegas ever got grocery baskets. And don't nobody ever come in here tryna buy enough to fill one. Most of this stuff's usually stale anyway. I learned that the hard way last time I craved some Fruit Loops. Tragic.

"Is this crystalized . . . or granulated sugar? Or . . . or is it pure CANE sugar?" I hear Old Man asking Bobby at the register from the next aisle. My guy is homeless with rich millennial taste. Must have made his rounds in Williamsburg. One time he fussed at Bobby for putting American cheese instead of cheddar on a bacon, egg, and cheese that I'd bought him. "'Cause the CANE sugar is the good shit. That's what I want in my coffee." Bobby eyeballs Old Man as I come down the aisle, ignoring his question. "And wheeeeere is the hazelnut half-and-half? I likes my coffee CREAMY."

I drop the juice, coconut water, and Pop's chips and gallons on the counter. "I got this and his coffee." Bobby mumbles something in Arabic as his eyes dart back and forth between the surveillance screen that hangs just above my head and Old Man, who's thumbing the coffee counter for a lid, still talking to whomever he thinks is listening about hazelnut half-and-half. Bobby is never not looking like he's worried and ready for somebody to steal something. Sometimes he barely even looks at me when I'm trying to hand him my money if somebody else is in there at the same time as me. But at least he don't got somebody sitting right outside the bodega in a wooden box facing the door watching every customer that comes out like the dollar store across the street does. At least this one don't got bulletproof glass we gotta speak into.

"All right, all right. Zas enough. Zas enough," he calls out to Old Man now that he knows I'm paying. He adds the cost of everything up out loud. A small kid who looks just like him barely peeks over

the counter and catches my eye from a stool he has perched just beyond the register. Behind his head is every kind of medicine, cigarette,
or household appliance anyone could ever need. Options are stacked
against the wall all the way to the ceiling. Pepto Bismol. Tylenol. Screw-
drivers. Durags. Newports. Milk of Magnesia. Nasty. "Twelve dollars,
baby. How you doing? No bacon and cheese? No cigarette?"

"I told you I don't eat dead animals no more, Bobby. And I don't
even know what you talkin' 'bout tryna sell me a loosie. I'm good," I reply.
I'm annoyed by his taunting smirk. Bobby asks me that almost every
time I come in here like it ain't been a whole year since I stopped eating
meat. It's annoying but at least he knows not to ask me about loosies
in front of Pop. Don't want him getting ideas. Grease snaps and sizzles
loudly on the griddle filling the cramped storefront with hot pig smoke.
I hand him the twenty and wait for him to count me back the change.

"Thank you, mama." Old Man raises his coffee cup to me as if to
toast to the only yes he's heard all day and makes his way out with Bobby's eyes glued on him until he's fully out the door. I grab the bag of
snacks and slide the gallons off the counter. I swear parents only have
us so they can use us helpless kids for cheap labor.

The Memorial Day weekend heat and sunlight pushes into my
face as I step out onto the sidewalk. At least five car speakers blast soca
from different directions throughout the neighborhood as I watch a
few motorcycles race down the orange fence-lined street. The block is
pressed for the careless vibes of summer life, with old ladies selling all
kinds of mini flags representing every Caribbean country on the map.
New fruit carts have popped up on the corner, jam-packed with sugar
cane stalks at least six feet high for families to suck on once the wet
heat turns the whole street into a West Indian block party. Dollar-cab
horns alert people waiting on the bus that they got room to give us all

a ride when the city fails us. Only two dollars for a ride up the street. Random police sirens enter the mix. Old Man is nowhere to be found.

———————

Stepping back into our fourth-floor apartment is like stepping out of a sweaty Jamaican bashment party scene into one of those old-folks smoke-filled jazz clubs Pop and Sandra probably met in forever ago. I hear the flit of random saxophone notes float from Pop's room and throw the chips on the counter. A thin stream of gray rises from a spliff-filled ashtray on the kitchen counter and I know there ain't no goin' back there now. He'll be fumbling around for at least the next three hours. Or until he starts getting on his own nerves. Bright side: The house smells only a little sour now and more like a steamed bar of soap. His musty work clothes are chucked somewhere I can't smell them. Also means I can chill on the couch with my phone in peace.

My phone vibrates and a notification flashes across the top of the screen. Tiff's name shows up as the screen opens to Facebook Messenger. It's about that time. Months have gone by and we're due, I guess.

Tiffany Harrison
WASSUP, CUZ? YOU MISS ME OR NAH?

Yaminah Okar
YOU MAD SILLY, GIRL, OF COURSE I MISSED YOU. EVERYTHING'S GOOD.
WASSUP WITH YOU??

Tiffany Harrison
LISTEN TO YOU. *MAD* SILLY. YOU THINK YOU REALLY FROM BROOKLYN
NOW, DON'T YOU? YOU CAN SAY *MAD* AND TALK LIKE CARDI B ALL YOU

WANT TO BUT YO ASS STILL GON' BE FROM OBSIDIAN. LMAO. BUT NAH,
THINGS IS COOL. I MEAN, EVEN WITH EVERYTHING GOING ON. YOU KNOW
HOW IT IS. YOU KNOW HOW EVERYBODY HANDLE STUFF AROUND HERE.

Never missing a chance to remind me of where I came from, this
is always how Tiff says hello. One part diss to New York. One part homage to the OB. One part family drama. One part envy that I got up out
of there unlike everybody else, including her.

Yaminah Okar
AND YOU WON'T EVER LET ME FORGET IT. AIN'T NOBODY
TRYNA FORGET. BESIDES I BEEN GONE FOR YEARS.
PRACTICALLY GREW UP HERE NOW.

Tiffany Harrison
OH, PLEASE. YOU STILL ONE OF US. BUT I GUESS I FEEL YOU, GIRL.
AIN'T NOTHIN HERE NO WAY. SEEM LIKE EVERYBODY JUST SAD ALL
THE TIME. I GET IT. I'M GLAD YOU GOOD. 'CAUSE I GOT SOME TEA. WELL,
MORE LIKE SOMETHING HAPPENING THAT I THINK YOU SHOULD KNOW.

I was waiting for this. Cousin Tiffany always has the tea.

Yaminah Okar
DO I REALLY WANNA KNOW? I'M TRYNA BE ON MY NAMASTE RIGHT
NOW. I DON'T KNOW IF I'M IN THE MOOD TO HEAR ABOUT SOMEBODY
ELSE IN THE FAMILY FIGHTING.

Tiffany Harrison
(...)

I see the dots on the screen that, for Tiff, means she's telling me whatever I probably don't want to hear anyway. My question completely rhetorical in her book. I wait for her to flesh out a full-on story about how Aunty Jo was rude to Cousin Jay's girlfriend again or how one of the neighborhood women tried to sabotage Nana's Sunday-dinner business. It's all happened before. Very little would surprise me at this point. Pop's saxophone squeaks from behind his closed door followed by him releasing a sudden cuss into the air. He's gonna need a break after that one. His door flings open and Tiff's message finally sends a link to an event.

YOU'RE INVITED TO THE WILLIAMS-JOHNSON 2019 FAMILY REUNION
IN MEMORY OF OUR SISTER
SANDRA ANNE WILLIAMS (SEPTEMBER 3, 1973—JANUARY 8, 2019)
OAK COMMUNITY PARK
Thursday, July 4—Sunday, July 7, 2019.
Are you going?
Yes   No   Maybe

Tiff's message bubbles pick up again. I read the Facebook invite title over again. Then again. Then a third time. You can receive an invite for anything on Facebook. Prom-posals. Graduations. Celebrations of death. Family get-togethers for families that have been broken since the beginning of time. *Are you going?* People have even been known to go live into the delivery room reeking of vagina blood while their best friend was pushing out a slimy-ass baby.

Tiffany Harrison
I FIGURED UNCLE JAMES FORGOT TO SEND YOU
THE INVITE AGAIN THIS YEAR

Tiffany Harrison
YOU STILL THERE?

I close Messenger, stuff my phone into my pocket, and walk over to the kitchen, where Pop leans over the counter, shoving handfuls of garlic plantain chips into his mouth. Crumbs fall into the gray hairs of his struggling goatee without him noticing. He washes it down with water straight from the jug, small streams escape down the sides of his face as he gulps with his head tilted all the way back, eyes closed. Pop might be the king of escape. For those few minutes it almost looked like that water was all that ever existed and he wasn't being dragged by the stress of this city.

"It's all these damn buildings that got my head all screwed up. I know it," Pop says, staring off into nowhere. "All these musicians moved to New York City to follow they dreams but ain't no nature in this dump! I used to be good, man. But these exhaust fumes is going straight to my brain. You know what Coltrane used to say? He said, 'All a musician can do is get closer to sources of nature.' But I'm convinced even them birds we be hearin' outside is bots, Minah. Can't even convince me them trees on the next block is real. I used to have something. I used to be able to play my songs, man."

If I just stand still, it'll be some other random day where Pop is just fussing as usual. Nothing special. Nothing going on. If I just stand still here for a while, Pop will be back in his room playing off-key and I'll be chillin' on the couch reading my horoscope, able to breathe.

"Minah. Did you hear what I said? Your pop is losing out here, baby girl."

In Memory of Sandra Williams. Date of death: January 8, 2019.

Sandra has been dead for four months. Does he know about Sandra? Plantain chip bits are sitting on Pop's gray hairs just under the drops of water he still hasn't wiped away. I feel the coolness of the countertop tiles under my damp hands now stuck here like glue. My one-hundred-pound hands. The crumbs start to blur like one big orange blob on the side of Pop's face, dancing up and down. They move around the same spot that words are coming out of but that I suddenly can't hear. Dark Brown. Black. Orange. Gray. A breeze flies over my eyes and I blink the water away. It slides down my face and wets my neck. Pop's face comes back into focus.

"Minah, baby. Are you there?"

Am I here? I run to my room and shut the door before Pop can say anything else.

Less than a minute later Pop's voice pleads on the other side of my bedroom door. Other days I would have feared for my life walking away while he was talking to me and even worse for slamming my door. Sandra has been in the ground since it was covered in snow and people were still wishing each other Happy New Year. What the fuck. My phone buzzes again against my thigh. I slide it back out from my pocket to see five more messages from Tiff. It doesn't matter that I'm not there. She'd continue talking to a wall if no one was there to listen to her run her mouth. I unlock it and open back up to click the link and read the rest of the Facebook invite:

Come join us as we celebrate family, our late sister Sandra, and our Lord and Savior Jesus Christ for the life He's given us and for keeping us together as a family. Cancer can try to break us down but the love of God keeps us up! Contact James Williams with your shirt size and Venmo $20 for your T-shirt by June 15th. Stay tuned for itinerary. Praise God!

Our Lord and Savior. Cancer. Sister Sandra. Jesus Christ. T-shirt. Praise God.

"Minah, baby. Come on and talk to your pop. Can't just go running off into your room like this. You scaring me. Come on now. What's this about?" Pop still pleads gently on the other side of the door. The windows shudder as a semitruck rolls by, two drivers downstairs lay on their car horns much longer than necessary. An ice cream truck's theme song plays off down the street and my phone buzzes again. I squeeze my eyes shut, blinking out the water, lift my body from against the door and jump back to my feet.

"Did you know about the family reunion this year, Pop? Did anyone tell you?" Pop and I stand face-to-face at my now-open doorway, sweat gathering over every inch of my skin. We have a lot of talks right here. Pop don't ever walk all the way in my room. Always talkin' about how a girl should have her space and I agree. "I got a Facebook invite from Tiff today. It says it's happening in July, Pop. You know anything about it?" Pop stares back at me, looking confused by the question while looking like he doesn't want to be caught in a lie. Sweat pools above his eyebrows, too. His bald head glistens just before he wipes a thick sheet of it away, taking a deep breath before he answers.

"That's what this is about? You know they have them things every two years and you haven't wanted to go to either of the two that went by since we left."

"So you knew!"

"Yeah, Minah. Your uncle told me about it. He still does even though you won't talk to nobody" is all Pop says, staring down at his hands. His hands still look strange without a wedding ring even though he took his off years ago. Sometimes he still slides his right thumb and middle finger over the space where it would be had everything not changed. "I didn't think you'd want to go or nothin' like that, Minah. You told me you were done with that side of the family. Told me you didn't wanna hear nothin' else about 'em," he continues softly. "You mad 'cause you think they didn't invite you?" he asks, finally looking me directly in the eyes.

"Did you see this invite, though, Pop?" I ask, getting hotter by the second. "It's not just another reunion. It's for . . . They said that . . ." The rest of what I try to say snags in the bottom of my throat like a deep crack in the street. The words are so big they feel like they'd choke me if I tried to make them come out.

"You know your pop don't have Facebook, Minah. James called me on the phone," he replies with a look on his face that I don't understand. Does he even know?

Does he know my mama is dead?

idn't nobody know what was about to hit Obsidian when it showed up. They say all of a sudden it started takin' over all the parties and then out of nowhere everybody was goin' crazy for it. We ain't never seen nothin' like it so it was strange how it became something everybody was cool with—no questions asked about where it came from. Somehow, we all just decided it was what everybody wanted to be around and no one disagreed. None of us knew what could happen when it came around except that it made the hood feel good. Made everybody forget they whole world and the pain in it. Made everybody forget what they own name was. Made everybody act out even on they own family. Do things they said they'd never do. It wasn't that expensive, but before we knew, it seemed like there was never enough money for all the times we wanted to go back for more. "I would never" turned into "might have to." And shoot, why not. And don't look at me like that, just let me hold something till tomorrow. I'll pay you back. You know I'm good for it. Nobody asked questions so it took time to notice how it made us go missing. Into the depths of dark alleys. Under the overpass before kids were even up getting ready for school. Down the street from the cookouts, "right quick" turning into days. It was mystical like that. So quick and powerful nobody saw it coming. Made you feel like fingers was wrapped around your neck but kept you begging for a tighter squeeze. Would creep up in your blood, stiffen, leave you in the same place for so long you forget who you are. Forget any reason you ever had for being alive.

TWO

Yesterday, Co-Star said it would be a day for a visit from the past. That I should be open to a surprise that'll make me think about how the old days are making it possible to understand the new. That when the past comes walking back into my life, I should look at it as a chance to exercise how much I've grown and acknowledge where I came from. That the past is a gift to the present. No wonder why Pop be looking at me crazy when I start talking about retrograde and alignment and rising signs and shit. Astrology is mad weird. But for some reason it makes me feel calm. Ever since Pop and I left and started moving around, I been needing things to make sense. He laughs at everything I do but he never explains anything. On a good day he'll call it hocus-pocus mess and tell me to cast a spell on his boss so he can get a raise. On all the other days, he acts like everything's cool but I know something's wrong with him, too. Horoscopes might not be real but at least it seems like whoever it is that's been studying the stars understands me. Or people like me, I guess. At least, unlike my family, somebody out there has some answers that feel a little like the truth.

But the thing is, don't nobody ever really tell the truth. And by nobody, I mean all the grown folks. Always keeping secrets 'cause they think we can't handle it. Think we too young to be honest with, so they tell us lies and stories tryna make everything seem all good when it ain't. They think our brains is too small to compute real life. Then they play dumb when you find out. Or they act like it's none of your business. They act like you couldn't possibly understand what's going on because life isn't a fairy tale like the books say. Like all the books you read in school filled with white girl princesses and happy slaves, pleased to serve their masters. But even worse—most of the time they just treat it like it's all a joke. Like it's no big deal. Like we all somehow just get over it and that none of us is in pain. Like we haven't been looking around. Like we all just keep it moving until we're gone.

I wait until it's all the way dark out again and Pop thinks I'm asleep. My light's been out since before the sun went down so it's believable. With only the glow from my phone lighting the space around me, I sit up from the dampness of my bed and toss it aside. It's been five hours and there's nothing left in it for me to research how we got here. I scrolled all the way back in my texts only to remember I deleted them years ago, my eyes swollen, tired of tears and staring into the black hole of blue light. Pins and needles attack my toes and then shoot up my legs as I stand to cross the room. I give my legs a minute to wake up. A gentle turn of the doorknob confirms that the door is locked and nobody can come in. Nobody's ever really tried but it always makes me feel better to know they can't even if they did. I open my closet door, tug on the chain hanging from the ceiling, and pull down the empty Reebok box.

The faint glow of the shady bulb gives enough light for me to sit on the floor and open the box I been keeping since we moved here. To a random person it'd seem like it's filled with a lot of goofy shit that don't mean nothing to anybody, but I know different. And nobody knows it's here anyway so it don't matter what they think. Lifting the lid, my hands move through old birthday cards, movie tickets, family pictures from before Instagram existed, and I smile a little bit at all the memories of times when I was happy. When we were really happy. Under those, all my love notes from Mike. Postcards mailed from the Bronx. Poems scribbled on the napkins from the Dominican restaurant off 181st Street. Drawings of the side of my face scribbled on receipt paper saved from the first time he took me to Coney Island. A photo-booth picture of us making funny faces at each other and the camera. Mike is corny like that. Corny enough to always be sending me things and telling me I can talk to him about anything. *"Anything,"* he says.

I move through old pictures of Pop and Sandra when I didn't exist yet, and Sandra had that look in her eye like she clearly was the baddest bitch and her man knew it. One picture of me on the day she taught me how to ride a bike on Jarvis Street, whole body covered in cushioning—knee pads, elbow pads, helmet—so I wouldn't die if I lost control and flew out into oncoming traffic. A whole hot mess. A bent corner of a photo watermarked KODAK with the words *Us, 2003* on the back juts out from under a big stack of unopened cards from Nana. I push the stack aside to turn the old photo right side up. There stands Pop in front of a big old house—our house—with both arms reaching around the sides of Sandra's belly, three times too big for the dress she's wearing but they're both smiling facing the same direction like they was taking a prom picture. Sandra's small hands rest just on top of Pop's, nails painted her signature purple, with long box braids flowing over her shoulders, over his tattooed arms, and down her back. The house looks different from the way I remember it. Maybe because I wasn't alive yet and that's back when things was better.

Pop's feet shuffle out of his room and close his bedroom door just before his footsteps get louder and louder like they're coming to my door. On Sundays, Pop plays at Fat Cat. I don't move until I hear the front door open and close again with the sound of his keys clashing against two of the three locks, making sure I'm safe. I flick more photos around and touch the corner of a teal American Spirit pack that appears under all the memories. I pull it from under, letting all the pieces of our family that I keep fall aside, and unlock my phone.

Me

where u at?

♥Mike♥

just left work . . . wyd?

Me

nothin' . . . sittin' on the floor.

♥Mike♥

sound like some emo shit. Lol what you wearin'?

Me

Lolol. shut up. can i see u? can u come get me?

A fresh set of tears begins to fall as I send the last text to Mike, turning the screen into a blurred glow of wordless light. I catch some just before they can drench the screen and just after he responds with a *yea*. I'm glad he can't see me yet or didn't have to hear my voice while I make this request. You can type *LOL* and send heart-shaped emojis in a text without anybody knowing that you're sad. Or that anything's wrong with you. You can type anything without the person on the other end knowing what's really up. Mike tells me he can meet me at the bus stop right by the Utica Avenue train station in an hour before telling me that he missed me. I wipe more tears away while I type *ok* and a *me too*, followed by a heart emoji and a wink.

THREE

Mike's neck is a damp combination of goose bumps, salt, and the frankincense oil he buys from the Muslim store down the street. I love it.

He holds still when I run my tongue across it with his back pressed against his bedroom door under my weight. I barely notice when he drops his hand behind him and locks it. I know he's too smart to ever let his mama catch us slipping. I hear the latch enter the hole and watch the edges of his lips curl up, pleased with himself as always. I wouldn't ever dare tell Pop that Mike's mustache easily beats his. He'd just wonder how I was even standing close enough to a dude like him to notice. I sound too much like a giddy little girl when the thick hairs tickle my face, pressed to his. This is my second time here. Behind a closed door with him. A locked door. I back away from it and sit on his bed.

"Come here," I command.

"Oh, you just gon' tell me what to do in my room, huh?" he questions, eyelids lowered, sizing up the situation. Mike always looks smacked. Pop would never believe me if I told him he don't even smoke.

"You actin' like you don't want to."

"I ain't say all that." Mike grazes his mouth with his pointer finger and thumb like he's wondering something before inching forward. I pull him onto me the minute he's within arm's reach. His bed is softer than I imagined. Ugly though. I don't know what it is about dudes and these comforters that look like they're about to go camping. Most of the ones I know ain't been hunting a day in their lives but all their beds look like somebody's granny ripped the shirts off hunting-ass white boys and made blankets with it. I know because most of them is too dumb not to take selfies with their bedrooms as a backdrop just before posting it on Instagram. I'd always sat on a chair or the floor until today.

I open my mouth and legs as he falls on top of me, pushing my tongue into his. My best friend Nikki coached me on this. She said to use lots of tongue and that he'd like it if I sort of tried to eat his lips.

He goes with it.

What I love about Mike is how he don't be askin' me no stupid questions. If I tell him I need to get out, he makes it his job to see me. And I needed to get out today. He knows Pop ain't cool with us runnin' around together, so we always meet somewhere neutral and discreet before our dates. Neutral and discreet equals Nikki. Pop don't really like her neither, but something about her is nonthreatening. Probably 'cause she's a girl. And maybe 'cause she's always been the one to look out for me in this city. You'd think by now that Pop would have caught on that girls can be plottin', too. Mike and I been seeing each other only a little over three months. Nikki knew him from her job and introduced us.

"What you doin', Yaminah?" I like that Mike uses my full name when he talks to me but this time I can hear suspicion in his tone.

"What does it look like? Taking off my shirt. Are you gon' help or what?" This is my attempt at seduction. Mike hovers over my face looking confused. I don't understand why he needs to question this or why he'd even want to be talking right now. This isn't how this was supposed to go. I pull my T-shirt off myself and pull his face back to mine. Lots of tongue. Lots of tongue. Sort of eat the lips.

"Yo, you trippin' right now." Mike unlatches me from his body and pushes himself up. My eyes catch his fallen fitted cap next to me on the bed and then scan the back of his head, his back still turned to me. Mike says his mama braids his hair, but I don't think she's touched that head since before we really started talking. "Yo, why you all over me all of a sudden?" The way Mike uses the word *yo* always feels like he's saying somethin' that's been on his chest for a long time.

"What you mean, 'all of a sudden'?"

"You ain't even really talk to me like that when we was walkin' over here. Barely even looked at me on the train. And last time you said you wasn't ready. Now you lickin' me and bitin' me and shit?" Mike slaps the back of his right hand into the palm of his left hand whenever he's trying to be serious with somebody. I don't want serious right now, though. I don't want to talk about nothin' unless it's what he wants to do to my body. I need him to touch my body right now.

"I don't know what you're talking about. Can you just come back over here? Don't you want me?" I plead.

"Of course I do. But . . ." He hesitates.

"But what? You don't want to be close to me?" For a minute Mike just stands there looking sad and doesn't speak. I drop my head down and focus on my hands to avoid the water trying to pool behind my eyelids. I read somewhere that people can read palms and tell things about the future and about past lives. I wonder now if somewhere in my palms it can tell me how my mama still has the power to make me feel like something's missing even when she's dead. Mike's body is close to mine again, where I need it, but this time sitting beside me, my right hand pulled tightly into his left. Silent. "I don't wanna cry about her no more, Mike." I don't have to tell him who "her" is. I only had to tell him about her once and he never made me have to explain again.

"But you ain't gotta fake for me, Minah. If you need to cry, go'on head and let it out," he says softly, keeping his gaze forward. I can tell when he's looking at me and when he's trying hard not to. I know when he doesn't know what to do but hold my hand. "I won't even trip if you get snot on my T-shirt." Tears and laughter gush from my face at the same time and I let myself fall over into the space between the ball of his shoulder and neck that he's made for me. I like how Mike ain't afraid of tears but don't let me stay sad for too long without sayin' nothin'.

"You remember when I told you about Tiff?" I start.

"Yeah. Your play cousin on your mama's side, right?" I've never told Mike that Tiff is my play cousin, but I guess he figured it out when I told him about how she just used to be around all the time when we was kids. She don't really belong to none of my aunties or uncles, but Nana been treating her like one of us ever since she came back to her house with me one day after we spent hours scraping our knees and playing tag on the playground. She's lived down the street from Nana's house my whole life and you wouldn't be able to tell the difference except she was lucky enough to get to go home at night.

"She sent me a Facebook message earlier today. Another family reunion's coming up this summer and she sent me the invite on there since she knew Uncle James didn't send it to me. You want to see it?" Before Mike can respond or wonder why I'm crying over a Facebook invite, I pull my phone out and push it into his hands, opening the screen to Messenger, scrolling up before all the messages Tiff sent afterward that I still won't read.

"Fuck." Mike reads fast. "Why ain't nobody tell you this before?" A rhetorical question I obviously don't know the answer to. Mike shakes his head and stares at the phone as if staring a little longer will help him find the thing inside of it that I'm missing. He scrolls further down to read the full description in silence and pauses to look up at me. "You okay?" Who would be? He pauses to lick his lips and looks away. "I mean, I know she used to treat you kinda wild but, like . . . that's your mama." I laugh before realizing how silly it makes me look.

"Of course they wouldn't tell me. They probably thought I ain't wanna know. I mean, I don't know if I wanted to know. Cancer?" The laughter erupts from my belly so forcefully that I'm scared I won't be able to stop. "Like, how HILARIOUS is that?!" Mike doesn't speak. He places one hand on my back, and my body shoots up from the bed at his touch. "Kind of makes sense, you know? She was so mean to me. Out of nowhere. How long can you treat your own fuckin' kid like you hate them and get away with it?" I now say through streaming tears. "Maybe since she ain't have me to take things out on no more, it all stayed inside her and finally ate up her body for good."

"Minah."

"I mean it, Mike," I explain, laughing again. "That's what the fuck she gets!" Before I know it, I'm throwing things that aren't mine, tipping over crates of books and video games, grabbing pillows, and swinging them into walls as hard I can. I start to swing so hard I lose balance and my legs are no longer beneath me. Somehow Mike softens the fall. "She just thinks she can ruin my life and then go die? She can just leave like that without telling me? Sounds very on-brand!" Mike pulls me from the floor all the way into his arms. I cash in on my permission to soak his shirt with everything pouring from my face.

"I'm sorry, Minah." He says the only thing he knows to say.

Sorry for my loss.

FOUR

If I were to rank offenses punishable by death in Pop's mind, spending the night at my boyfriend's house would probably be at the top of the list. But between all the energy crying took from me and having to face the 4 train in the Bronx after midnight, dealing with what Pop might have coming for me was a chance I had to take.

So I stared at the cement walls of Mike's cramped bedroom as he held me through the night before walking me to Mount Eden, the closest stop to where he stays but almost the last stop on the green line. Already groups of Dominicans hovered over the curb with their car doors open to the sidewalk blasting reggaeton and puffing from their community hookah, small chairs posted up for all their friends to come kick it. It's eight in the morning and Memorial Day. Far before noon the sidewalk is a developing party. The whole neighborhood creating its own theme song bouncing off its high, Pepto Bismol-colored building walls. Mike walks coolly beside me on the street side, pressing his knuckles gently into the small of my back whenever it's time to turn.

"I know where we're going," I snap softly. Usually Mike's gestures make me feel special and safe, but today I can't help but feel like a charity case that he's treating like a box marked FRAGILE. He nods, saying good morning to the neighborhood grandmas sitting on their small stoops, and stops to hold the door open for one pushing a full cart out of CTown. The fact that he always gotta be so kind to every-body gets on my nerves sometimes.

"I know you do" is all he says after a few moments pass. The sidewalk curves and swoops down past a busy laundromat marked WASH AND GO in white lettering surrounded by a loud shade of blue. Across from it, the Dominican spot Mike's taken me to before is still open from last night and full with people behind a steamy display window leaning into foggy glass placing their orders for plantain, rice and beans, and stewed pork. Fencing shakes to the left of me as a basketball flies into it from across the court. I wince even though I know it's already been stopped by the metal. Mike slides his hand farther across my back and reaches his arm around my waist, pulling me in closer.

"I'm okay, Mike. I'm good," I lie. Because what is he even gon' do about it? He keeps his eyes forward, saying nothing until we reach the corner just across from the subway stairs.

"Look, I know you gonna keep acting like all this don't mean nothing to you, like it's no big deal, but you don't gotta act like that. I don't know what I would do if I just found out what you just found out, Minah." He pauses and looks around as a mother walks behind us, holding tight to her son. With his free hand he clutches the strap of his Black-Is-King backpack sagging off his shoulders that's almost the same size as his body with a snot stream trailing from his nose down to his upper lip, his small legs trying to keep up. "Just text me when you get to your house, okay?" I nod yes before he pulls me in for a hug and smushes a kiss into my cheek. I hear the rumble of the 4 train coming down the tracks above me and run.

The mornings after Pop plays Fat Cat he sleeps in until noon. It'll take me at least an hour to get back down to Crown Heights with no train delays, and ain't no guarantees that won't happen, especially since it's a holiday and that's only one of the one million things that could make the train be on some silly shit. I make it up the stairs onto the platform just in time to catch the doors open and drop into a seat as the doors close behind me and the subway theme song plays, "Stand clear of the closing doors, please." The fact that the announcement says please even though it'd close on that ass if you tried to hop on a few seconds too late is hilarious but don't nobody ever find it funny.

"LADIES AND GENTLEMEN . . . Excuse the interruption. Pardon me. I don't mean to bother you. This is embarrassing for me. But I ain't ate in five days . . . I'm homeless . . . and I got three kids to feed. I lost my job three months ago and me and my family been struggling to get back on our feet. We lost everything. I applied for food stamps yesterday and I just need a little change to get something to eat and buy milk and Pampers for my baby girls." The man shuffles his feet down the middle of the train car with a limp and a toe sticking out of one of his busted sneakers. His jeans look like he's been rolling around in dirt and he's got on way too many layers for us to be just a few weeks away from summer. "I ain't tryna bother nobody. We just goin' through a real hard time. If you could spare a dollar, a quarter, a nickel, or even a penny to help me and my family out . . ."

A white man in a cheap business suit who don't look like he's supposed to be on this train drops a few coins into his cup, pauses and smiles awkwardly, looking around him while most of the people on the train try not to make eye contact. "God bless you. If anyone else could spare a dollar, a quarter, a nickel, or a penny to help my family *eat* today . . ." He pauses in front of each person he passes repeating the same line meant to make us all feel bad for his hunger. This is when it becomes peak time for everybody to scroll through their phones looking at nothing in particular, reading books that weren't gonna be opened, or pretending to sleep extra hard. I search my back-pack for headphones for the third time and realize again that I forgot them at home last night in my hurry to meet Mike. I didn't need them on the way to his house and now I hate myself for forgetting. I never leave the house without my headphones for moments like this. And now the homeless man is paused in front of me expecting change. I freeze and stare at the floor, breathing through my mouth to avoid the smell of piss that I know he wears like the cheap cologne the dudes at my school be wearing. If I ignore him long enough, he'll keep it moving to the next person.

When me and Pop moved to Crown Heights five years ago, Pop taught me the rules of riding the subway quick. Sometimes he came here for gigs back in the day so he knew some things that I ain't know about getting around a big city. Specifically New York. Like how you can't respond to every homeless person who asks for something on the street. And that not all of them are "just" homeless. Pampers and baby formula most definitely meant something else according to Pop. How you can't just be walkin' around with your phone out and money in your hand. How you can't be caught slipping on the train because anything could pop off at any given moment. He'd tell me I'd better have something constructive to do 'cause I'm probably gon' be sitting there for a long time, stuck stuffed between all those people. And "some of them ain't gon' be wearing deodorant," he'd warn me.

Back then I thought he was being dramatic, 'cause we had homeless people back in Obsidian. And the rest of the rules just sounded like common sense if you live in *any* city. But ain't no city like New York City. And there definitely ain't no place like Brooklyn. So I learned soon enough that Pop was right about how I needed to handle myself when I left the house and when I got on the train. I minded my business and kept to myself in general. Pop still told me that I needed to stay alert but I added wearing headphones on the list, too, once I realized I couldn't walk down the street in my neighborhood without dudes tryna holler at me. Or walk down the street without having to ignore homeless people and addicts when I ain't have nothing to give. But I was smart enough to know not to do that at night.

Six stops down I can tell we're not in the Bronx no more. Right before my eyes the car shape-shifts into a confetti of skin colors and weird lives. Everybody got somewhere to be, even when it's a holiday, and we become smooshed into one another's bodies tryna get there. The air is a hot, thick steam of random breath-and-skin smells that make me want to throw up right here in front of everybody. Pop used to tell me that I'd get used to it. That if I just mind my business like everybody else, I'd forget how nasty this place is and one day see the magic and the beauty, as he called it with his eyes glazed over, always looking far off at something that wasn't there. But ain't enough business in the world that's gon' make me unsee all the hands that's touched that pole in the middle of this train car. Fingers that's been digging all up in people's nasty-ass noses.

A baby next to me lets out a scream that cracks the air around us all and its mama starts searching like crazy for something to make it stop before anybody has the chance to look down on her. She finds its pacifier and its eyes get all big and just stare back up at her as it sucks on plastic nothingness. She smiles back at it like ain't nobody else in the world. Even with all these people crowded around our seats, arms holding on to the rail just above our heads. She notices me staring and presses the child deep into her chest as if I'm the biggest threat on this train. I wonder if she posts pics of her baby on Instagram.

It's hard to remember Sandra from back when she used to look at me and hold on to me like that. Before Pop and I moved out of Obsidian for good and left everybody behind, including her. There used to be pictures all over our old house of us together. Sandra watching me crawl around with my cousins on the kitchen floor. Sandra adjusting that expensive, itchy-ass dress her and Pop made me wear for Christmas when I was two. Sandra wiping some unknown food-thing off my face with her spit and the back of her thumb. My eyes begging Pop to come from behind the camera to save me from the weird things she'd do because I was too little to do it myself. It's hard to believe that same person is in the ground now and ain't nobody tell me when it happened. Did they think I was still that little girl I was before we left Obsidian who everybody whispered around? Did they think I wouldn't understand her being sick? Did they think I wouldn't care?

The 4 train pulls into the Crown Heights–Utica Avenue stop, and the loud voice over the intercom screams at us about clearing the train because it's the last stop. Standing in front of the doors, waiting for them to open, I cringe at my reflection. Swollen eyelids beneath a cascade of old Marley twists that I ain't bother to force into a ponytail high above and away from my face like most days. I should fix that before Pop think too much about what was going on wherever I went last night. The homeless dude cuddled into the corner on the opposite end of the car snorts, scratches his ass, and switches to his left side facing the back of the seat but don't wake up, unmoved by the chance that MTA police is gonna kick him out of his temporary home as soon as these doors open.

It feels like I've been asleep this whole ride, wishing I could wake up from the nightmare inside my head. Just days ago I wasn't even thinking about her and now I can't stop seeing her face every time I close my eyes or sit still for more than a few seconds. And how am

I supposed to walk into my house now? Pop is usually still asleep around this time but he's a different person when he's worried. He should have thought about that before he chose to keep this from me. Before he decided to treat me like a child who always needs to play pretend like everybody else.

———

"Good morning, Munch." Pop calling me by the nickname he gave me when I was three feels like somebody's hand reaching into my chest and squeezing as hard as they can, then letting go and running away. He wasn't supposed to be awake yet and here he is sipping coffee out of a bodega cup on the couch with the TV off like he's been there all night. By the steam I can see that the coffee's hot so I know it hasn't been that long since he went across the street to snoop around. He only goes over there when he wants to know where I've been. Otherwise he sends me to deal with Bobby myself.

"Hey." Maybe if I disguise my fear of what comes next after being caught sneaking in in the morning with some righteous anger, whatever's next won't come. Maybe if I say as little as possible, Pop won't treat me like his daughter who slept somewhere he doesn't know about without permission and, instead, he'll treat me like the daughter he's been lying to. Maybe he'll beg for my forgiveness. Maybe he'll do something like that.

"All you got to say is 'hey'? Where you been at all night, huh?"

"I—I went for a walk, Pop." He had to have gone to sleep. He couldn't have been up all night and this morning. He's not thinking about this backpack I got on, I think.

Pop looks over at my bedroom door as if his eyes were a finger pointing at my mistake. I'd left it cracked by accident in my rush to leave. Stupid. "Try again." The words are said quietly but forced through his clenched teeth. A sign that he's trying to be patient but don't have too much left.

"Okay. I—I was with Nikki. I know I should have—" I begin to lie again through my twists that I'd forgotten to pull back before walking through the door, eyes digging into my shuffling sneakers still just inside the front door.

"Maybe you should have told her where you was gon' be before you used that lie." Our eyes meet: mine probably too big to continue the story I was trying to produce out of thin air. His, searching me through deeply judgy, furrowed brows. "She was across the street picking some things up for her mama while I was getting this coffee. She ain't say nothing about you. But you wasn't with her, Munch. Now, I'ma give you one last chance," he says, leaning forward, arms resting on his knees as he turns his full body in my direction to look into me. "You wanna tell me where you was really at all night, or are we gon' keep playin' these games?" He looks away again at nothing in particular in front of him and takes a slow, tired breath. The regular blare of sirens coming down the street vibrates through the walls in our silence and the honks of back-to-back dollar vans follow. I stand there not knowing what lie to tell for what seems like forever. It doesn't matter where I was. I didn't do anything and I'm not the one walking around with anything to hide, anyway.

"Mike's." The hand from before comes back to reach into my chest and squeezes even harder this time. Pop chuckles and nods his head looking down into his coffee cup, then caresses it like it's the face of a baby he was suddenly stuck with. He leans forward.

"Well, check you out. Out here spending the night with your lil boyfriend like a grown-ass woman, huh? You paying bills, too?" Here

we go. Pop's sarcasm gets on my nerves. It's not like I've ever done anything like this before. He doesn't even bother asking questions before
he assumes he knows what I was doing over there. Pop stands up and
comes closer to me, where I've yet to move from before all this ques-
tioning started. I take one step back, closer to the door. "I know what
teenage boys are like, Munch. I was one be—"

"Why didn't you tell me, Pop?"

"If that boy hurt you, I'll—"

"About Sandra!" When Pop is standing this close to me, I have to
look up to make eye contact. He ain't no giant, but he's got a whole foot
on me. His tall frame shrinks to my five foot, three inches when her
name spews out of my mouth like vomit. His jaw flexes beneath his
stubbled cheek. Suddenly, his eyes look like they supposed to be in a
doll's face, made of glass, and locked on something too far away. Somebody might think I'm pulling a move by changing the subject, but who
gives a fuck where I was at, honestly. This is what I need to know.

"Munch—"

"Please don't lie, Pop. Please don't lie about this." My keys press
deeper into my palm as my hands form a tight fist around them.

"I'm sorry, baby."

"I'm not a baby. Why ain't nobody tell me, Pop?"

"Well, it's complicated, ba—Munch. I—I wanted to tell you so
many times but you get so mad every time I bring her up. I didn't want
her causing you no more pain. It's a lot to explain. It's too much." Pop
looks even sillier to me now than he did when I first walked into the
house. His oversized button-up paired with the old baseball cap that
he barely ever takes off his head, his forever gig uniform no matter the
venue. Every time he pushes his hand into his face to rub his struggle
beard, I hear sandpaper.

"'Too much'? For who? I'm sixteen years old. Not six. How long did you know she was sick?"

"Well, Munch, that's—"

"People don't just up and die from cancer without somebody knowing about it, Pop! HOW LONG DID YOU KNOW?!" Pop freezes and I'd be scared for screamin' on him any other day but he doesn't even look like somebody to be afraid of standing in front of me with a look I ain't ever seen before. "I read in the family reunion invite that Sandra had cancer. How'd she even get that, Pop?"

"Hmm . . . cancer. That's, uh, I don't know how anybody gets that, Minah." His eyes go big as he says this, right before he focuses them on the ground. He rubs his chin even harder this time like there's an equation scribbled into the floor that he wishes he could solve but already knows he can't. He looks like he was expecting me to say different words altogether.

"Not anybody. Her." Pop turns his back to me and walks over to the couch. It groans as he plops down into it where he'd been perched when I walked through the door. He leans over the coffee table, picks up his half-smoked spliff, lights it, and stares off at nothing after taking a long pull. He rests his hands, crossed, in his lap and shakes his head, letting the smoke seep slowly out of his nose. Just a few minutes ago I was the one being interrogated about where I was and what I'd been doin' all night, but now Pop looks like the one who's in trouble. Now he looks like the one tryna figure out what to say.

"Don't nobody know how it happens, Minah. All we know is that it don't seem like it cares too much about what it does to families." Adults know everything until they don't know shit. Convenient. He takes another drag, blowing the smoke back out, finally looking over at me. "Your mama was sick for a long time and you was already mad at her 'cause everything that happened . . . I . . . I ain't never had to break no news like that to you before without her being there to help me do it. I just . . ." His voice trails off and the empty look on his face makes me feel sorry for him. It's pitiful.

I stand there shifting, still in my sneakers, watching the smoke rise and fill our small Brooklyn apartment's stale air, spreading but having nowhere to escape to. I don't know what else to say to Pop, or even ask. I'm low-key disgusted by him not knowing what to say to me at a time that I got all these questions. I was the one kept in the dark all this time. I was the one who ain't nobody think could handle the truth, and here he is staring off with nothing to say. I used think Pop and Sandra knew everything. Always talkin' all low, laughing at some inside joke of theirs from behind the walls of our old kitchen in Obsidian like there was nothing too serious for them to handle in our house. But Pop just looks like any other person now—lost.

I look down at my sneakers and the space where I normally slide them off before placing them against the wall. I usually tuck them next to Pop's vintage Reebok 85s that he'd gotten at a random thrift store in the West Village when we first moved here. That day he'd told me we couldn't be caught out here in these mean New York streets without legit sneakers. I remember looking around at the feet of all the people who looked like they'd rushed off a runway to get to the next thing and felt like both of us definitely were underdressed. I knew buying new sneakers wouldn't change nothin' about how out of place we looked, though. We looked like what we were: a tall, scrawny-lookin' black dude just tryna hold it together and his standoffish kid stuck in the nineties from a simple-ass city learning how to live a whole new life. A whole new life in a place that could eat us alive if we ain't find a way to shake the sadness off us. That day we came home with new sneakers and two bags of groceries me and Pop lugged all the way from Manhattan 'cause we wanted to eat good our first week here. We learned fast that finding the fresh stuff in our new neighborhood was hit-or-miss. But Pop couldn't get the stove to work and we didn't even have a table to eat on yet anyway. So, that night we went to Sally's Diner.

Pop still tries to keep up our old Obsidian traditions by promising that we'll grill every holiday. And me not eating meat aside, being a butcher now meant he always came home with something fresh to cook up. Today we were supposed to brave the mystery of the back staircase that leads up to the dingy rooftop through a small door at the end of the seventh-floor hallway. "We can throw on some tofu dogs for you, or whatever you be eatin' at barbecues now," he'd said. But I could tell nothin' was getting grilled around here today as I hear my stomach's growls interrupt this standoff between me and Pop's lies.

"Pop?"

"Yeah, Munch."

"You hungry?"

"I could eat. And I can hear that stomach of yours screamin' from all the way over here." I drop my bag while Pop ashes what's left of his joint and slips on his sneakers before leading me out the door.

At first, won't nobody suspect nothing. They just gon' be jealous. Think you too caught up in your new lil friend to come around anymore. Think you too busy to remember your family to come out the streets and get home. Think all you ever want from them is money. Instead of being worried about you, they just get mad, you know? Won't ask too many questions besides where you've been and who you were with. They don't ask you how you doin' or if you need some help. Instead they'll see somebody different when they look at you. Somebody that they don't know. Say you gettin' a little too skinny. Assume you're doin' it all on purpose. Assume you're being hardheaded, livin' that fast life and all your new lil friends are just fast, too. They won't know that you'd eat if you could. That you wish it could be like it used to be but you can't help yourself no more, and the looks on their faces makes it hard to tell them the truth. They won't know that you're sick. At first, they'll call you everything else . . . but that.

FIVE

Nikki Joy is sparkling dust riding the air, coming into the shape of a human just behind my locker door minutes before the first bell rings.

I smell her first before I see her, and even after that, there's no time to figure out what combination of tropical fruits it is today. I close the green metal door, and two eyes dig into the side of my face, pressed for details as if we didn't talk just last night. Texting is talking and I already told the girl ain't nothing going on, but she don't ever believe me. She's queen of information, and she always gotta have it all when the tea is about me.

"My guy . . ." I pause to size up today's look. "How are you braving the weather in this? I know it ain't quite summer yet but shiny thigh-high rain boots? It's just school. Ain't nobody checking for all that." All of her five feet—five foot five in her black patent leather platforms—is leaned against the wall of lockers relaxed like class isn't starting in less than two minutes. She claims these boots help her look some-body in the eye if there's business to be handled. Or if she wants to send vibes to the next admirer in line. The look gets even more epic as you move above the knee where she's squeezed her thighs into a light blue denim miniskirt and matching denim jacket, which is open just enough to see a sunflower-print T-shirt on the inside. Cascading over and past her shoulders, picked-out curls that were tight against her head just a week before. She's pulled the top half of all this into two slicked-back buns that sort of look like horns if you squint your eyes a little bit.

"Now, you know that's a lie. Everybody is checking for *all* of this."

I lean back to check her out as she gives me a full turn so I can see her craftsmanship from all angles.

"I just had to tell one of your lil friends to leave me alone on my walk over here."

By *lil friends* Nikki means "boys," something she has no interest in as a whole. And as much as they act like her proud fatness is too much, they always seem to wish it was theirs. "Besides, it ain't just school. It's the world, Minah, the world. And I'm tryna be ready for it." Nikki's always talking about the world being her stage, her playground, or whatever new metaphor she can come up with when I point out that the glitter might be too much. "Are you ready for the world, Minah? I know the oversized T-shirt and I-don't-care-about-being-pretty-I-might-be-one-of-the-bois look is your thing, but damn."

"What are you talking about?"

"You just look . . . a little tired, fren. I thought we talked about this." The bell blares as we step into Ms. Dunham's classroom and she walks to close the door right behind us. We all know this means anybody on the other side of it is assed-out and has to go to the principal's for a pass since there's no way to open from the outside once it's closed. Me and Nikki are almost never late but Nikki calls lockouts a tool of the white-supremacist patriarchy's plot to keep the Black Man behind. I haven't read enough books to know what that means yet, but I know enough to know she means getting in trouble for being a few minutes late is oppressive. She's not wrong. A minute later Pierre Valentin tries to turn the doorknob, then shakes it when it won't open as if its being locked is a surprise. He does this every week, though. We all laugh as we watch him smoosh his face into the window like he's crumbling to his death, letting his face slide down the glass until Ms. Dunham blocks the view.

"I hope none of you plan to try that mess two weeks from now. You pull that stunt this time on June tenth and most of you can kiss your dreams of passing goodbye." The class explodes into a collective *Oooooo*, like Ms. Dunham played the entire junior class's life in a face-off right before the most highly anticipated fight. My whole body freezes when I realize she's talking about the end-of-the-year exhibitions. Nikki nudges me as if to say *see?* but I ignore her.

Ms. Dunham turns to face the board to write out a mock question that could be thrown out at us by a panelist to test our comprehension.

Traditional vaccines for diseases such as measles, polio, and influenza prepare the body to defend itself against future infections. These vaccines most often contain
(a) white blood cells
(b) antibiotics
(c) antibodies
(d) weakened pathogens

Google says that people with cancer can end up with fewer white blood cells. Google says humans need white blood cells for their immune system to be strong. Google says your immune system is the network of organs, cells, and proteins that help you fight off disease so you don't die.

"By a show of hands, who recognizes this question? Who can answer?" I hear the clock ticking. Pencils being flipped against tabletops.

Butts shifting in chairs. Hot breath loudly being pushed out of bored mouths. But nobody moves to raise their hand. Nobody wants to have to talk in front of everybody else. Even if they know the answer. Even Nikki would rather save her energy for something less depressing, while I just sit here feeling like I'm being trolled. Why is my teacher more ready to speak about the dead than my pops is? Whatever.

"Yaminah?" Ms. Dunham's voice is like a hand yanking me up out of a spell by the collar of my T-shirt. How could I forget? The easiest thing for a teacher to do in a class full of silent-ass kids is to call on the person who looks most off guard. Easiest person to put on the spot.

"Wha—ya—what was the question?"

She points to the board again. "What would you say if someone on the panel asked you this?" she presses, expecting me to give her something to help us all escape this awkward silence. I'd tell them that, whatever it is, clearly it's some shit that don't work for everybody. I'd say, it's some shit I don't believe in if people still die. But instead, I tell Ms. Dunham what I happened to be reminded of while I was up last night trying to understand.

"Weakened pathogens," I say, without lifting my chin off the arm I have stretched across my desk. She looks at me a second longer, like she's waiting for me to say more, and I hope she just moves on, 'cause that's all I got. Ain't nothin' else to say.

"Correct."

"They basically make viruses and stuff powerless . . . they make it hard for somebody to die from stuff 'cause they make you stronger. They recognize it when it tries to come back and fights against whatever is tryna make you sick again," Nikki chimes in, glancing over at me.

"Yo, boo, you deep as fu—"

"Language!" Ms. Dunham interrupts Jason, the class hype man, who's unfortunately landed a seat directly behind Nikki today.

"I'm just sayin', I like that in a shorty!"

Ms. Dunham's eyes cut in his direction long enough to halt another one of his weak attempts to get Nikki's attention. Usually he doesn't make it to class until just before the bell rings and the seat behind her is already taken.

"That's correct, Nicole. If we were to put you and Yaminah's answers together, that would be sufficient when you're standing in front of a panel, proving that you learned something in here." She pauses and looks back and forth between us and then looks around at the whole class. "But you're not gonna have one another so I suggest you all practice being able to answer, fully, for yourselves. Remember, answer the question and then back it up with information that supports your claim, like a definition."

"Yes, baby, pleaaaase, back it up for me," I hear Jason say under his breath. Nikki turns, pushing her curls back as she lowers her head and lets the gum she's chewing drop out of her mouth onto Jason's desk and smiles before facing back forward. He shrugs back in his seat, taking the hint for now.

Ms. Dunham goes on writing other questions that might come up during exhibitions as her voice lowers into the backdrop of my daydreaming. I stare past her back into the dusty chalkboard, seeing myself stand in front of a bunch of strangers ready to judge how much I paid attention in class all year. They'll be asking me scientific questions about bodies and stuff, and I can't even imagine myself telling them whatever it is that we learned in some book. Ms. Dunham turns around to face us, and I notice the bloodred shade of the lipstick she's wearing today. Then her mouth becomes bigger and bigger until all

I can see is red lips bouncing in slow motion. Every few seconds the lips open wider for a second and I catch smudges of red that have gotten caught on the front teeth. I'm sure I smell lavender, too, right when a gust of cool air rushes over me, and the calming scent is replaced by tropical fruits. Nikki's hand is on my shoulder and the class is empty.

"Girl, can we go now? The bell rang a whole minute ago and you been staring off into space somewhere like you not even here. We can't be late to math. I'm not tryna be caught out here, looking like Pierre's silly ass." Nikki looks confused but doesn't have enough time to be worried about wherever it is that I went. I wouldn't even be able to tell her if she asked. I pack up my stuff in silence and follow her out across the hallway. We're lucky, not having to go far for our next classes with all the mess that goes down in these hallways.

Nikki stops at her locker to check herself out in the mirror and switch out textbooks while I stand in the center of the hallway, looking up and around me like a dummy. I catch whiffs of bodies, raw like they've been out in the sun all day, brushing past me on their way to class or huddling in groups talking shit, pretending to care about making it to their next one on time. The air thick with all of us ready to be done for the year. The walls are covered with reminders about the last days of school: assemblies, senior yearbook dues, and exhibition requirements. Posters and sign-up sheets for things that all felt relevant up until two days ago.

I catch Nikki staring at me like a sad puppy dog, expecting me to quit acting weird. I walk into math before she has a chance to say anything. Clutching my books to my chest as I walk into a class of over thirty kids, the chaos pulls me in like a hug I hope keeps me invisible till the end of second period. Better yet, till the end of the day.

———

"Err'body got they pots at least halfway full?" A sprinkle of nods and peace signs tell him he can move on. "Good, good. Go'on ahead and cut on your stoves, turning the knob all the way high. Don't be scared." We hover over everything Kofi tells us that we'll need: one half carton of eggs, a large pot, a serving spoon with holes, a mini stove, and a sink. Walking between each table, he gives a whole speech about what it means to take care of something. How our hands need to be steady with our eyes focused. How we need to respect what's in our hands and protect it or it won't survive. Be gentle with it or it's gon' be yolk everywhere. Kofi's faculty ID says MR. WILLIAMS but he told us there ain't no Mister about him. Told us call him by his first name 'cause we all just here being humans together. Today that means we humans in home economics class learning how to poach an egg. Simple.

"All right now, so you gon' let that water get real hot," he explains, pausing to take a giant step closer to the center of the room. "When it comes to a boil, you ready for the next step. And who can tell me what we're about to do next? I know somebody can." Hands fly up all over the class and I shrink, hoping it'll be enough to distract him from mine not flying up with theirs. He pauses at my makeshift countertop and waits. "I see your hand, Pierre. Tell us what we need to do next, my man."

"Aight so *boom!*" Pierre slams his fist into his palm. "You gon' get you an egg, *nah mean*?! And you gon' grab you a utensil. I personally fucks with forks the most so I'ma get a fork, feel me?"

"Pierre?"

"My bad, Kofi. I personally *like* to use forks 'cause they hella heavy, you know?" Pierre's dramatics make it hard for him to move on until he gets some crowd participation, so he pauses to let Marcos and Anthony boost his ego the only way black Brooklyn boys in high school know how.

"Yeeeeerrr!"

"Aight!" Over the top and loud like we're outside competing with the sound of all the sirens going up and down Utica just blocks away. Who does this in class? Pierre daps them both up while somehow grazing his nonexistent mustache at the same time.

"So then, you gotta like—"

"THANK YOU, Pierre!" The way Kofi interrupts us sometimes don't ever really sound rude. It just sounds like your time is up 'cause we got things to do. Plus, none of us can stomach his voice for more than a minute, low-key. Everybody chuckles a little but not too much. "Atiya, what you got on it? Finish that step for us."

"I don't know," she says, pulling her shoulders almost up to her ears and dropping her head lower. Kofi calls on her every day like she doesn't say the same thing every time. Don't nobody know if she's telling the truth or what her problem is if she isn't, but Kofi has this weird way of believing everybody deserves a chance to be heard. Even if at first they think they don't wanna be.

"Why don't you give it a shot? Whatchu gon' do with the egg and, possibly, a fork? I know you know." At the beginning of this semester when we'd just met Kofi, this would have been the perfect moment for Pierre to debut another one of his fat jokes. An opportunity to tell Atiya she could sit on it. Call her a big bitch, a cow, a sloth, Most Likely to Take a Bite Out of the Big Apple. All things he called her first semester, every chance he got. But he only tried it once in home ec before he learned that Kofi don't play that shit in here. And that's why, for the first time all morning, I wasn't wishing I was anywhere else, by myself and alone to hear all these stupid feelings I ain't even know I had. Atiya shrugs again. "I crack it open and let it fall in the water."

I breathe out knowing since Atiya answered, there won't be so much pressure on me.

"Ayyyyyyye, what I say? Yes. Yaminah, bring us home. What do we do once we've *gently* cracked the egg and dropped it into the water?"

Fuck. I pick up one of my eggs, crack it over the water with a fork and pick up the holey spoon, dipping it into the water turning the water gently. The whites of the eggs start turning a bright white, twisting around the yellow ball of yolk in the middle like a tornado. The white starts to wrap and cover the yolk until my hand jerks and somehow the spoon swipes across the water and breaks the egg in half.

"Fuck, I killed it." I don't realize I said that out loud until Pierre screams, "EXPRESS YO'SELF," giving the whole class the cue to laugh. Looking up at Kofi, I don't see him at all. Instead it looks like a thing with the same colors on as him, reeking of nag champa like him, a thick ball of ropes at the top of his head like him. From memory I know the red circles around his eyes are frames and the large light beaming from his nose is a gold hoop and not the sun, even though it moves and shines when he moves if you're trying to look at it through a well of tears. The figure is asking me something. I still know it's Kofi the way it's moving its arms around while asking me something that sounds too muffled to make out until I blink. One swipe of the back of my hand brings me back into the room.

"Minah, would you like to take a break?"

"I'm good," I lie. Dots of water sit on top of my upper lip, my forehead, my chest. I feel it trickle down my back, my belly. I wipe my forehead with the back of my hand and complain, "It's hot as hell in here. Why they don't never have the AC on in this dump?" I ask no one in particular.

"Go on and take that break. Get you some water." He's telling me now. "Take a lap through the halls and some deep breaths. Come back when you're ready," he says, lowering his voice for the last part as if he's telling me a secret.

"Fine." Atiya watches me pass her desk to get to the door where the hall pass hangs next to it. She looks at me confused at how I've replaced her as the kid who needs breaks and deep breaths and permission to go cry somewhere nobody can see her. I pull the tie out my hair and let my twists cascade over my face, giving myself somewhere to hide on my way out the door. If I'm lucky, it'll disguise all the salt water mixing with the snot like a bubbling river stuck at the bottom of a waterfall.

———

The first time one of the fevers came over me I thought I was gon' die. Like I ain't know what was about to happen but I knew, whatever it was, it would be bad. Like, real bad. It was in the fifth grade. Almost the end of the year and I was the new kid at Bell Elementary 'cause Pop and I had to move suddenly. The minute I walked into class it was showtime. My first day and Ms. Hines was old and out of touch so she must have thought writing my name across the board for the whole class to see is what I wanted.

"Class, we have a new student. Y-A-M-I-N-A-H O-K-A-R," she spelled out carefully across the board in colossal-sized chalk letters. "Honey, did I spell it right?" I remember nodding quietly as I reached up to make sure my tight curls were still pulled back into the bun I'd tried for the first time that morning while scanning the room quickly for all possible enemies. It was the first time I'd done my own hair. "It's time for you to step up," Pop had told me that morning when Sandra didn't get up early enough to do it for me.

"ARE YOU OKAAAY, OKAAAR? Bwahahahahahaha!" A weak-ass joke the whole class used as an excuse to laugh obnoxiously. The laughing stopped under the slap of the giant notebook Ms. Hines had swiftly lifted above her head and brought down hard against her desk, the whole room stiffening to a shook hush.

"Class, let me remiiind you that we show new students *respect* in here," she warned through a curled lip I'd started to miss seeing on Sandra whenever she had been mad at me. Regular mad. Not the kind of mad she started getting right before we left the OB. "And if you can't do that, there's a seat for you in Mrs. Philip's office," she finished through her clenched teeth. I knew Ms. Hines had been doing her teacher thing by making them stop but it was too late. My pits were already dripping. It's probably why the kid whose name I didn't know yet cracked that stupid joke about me being okay. I wasn't okay. Beads of sweat were coming from everywhere and the random giggles were echoing in my head nonstop as if I were being haunted right there in front of everyone. Pop had told me to avoid drawing any attention to myself. That even though I was new and some kids might mess with me for having a different-sounding name, I should keep my head down and just do the work. Keep my head down. Do the work. No excuses. I was already a failure. "This is only until we can move for real this summer," he'd said.

I remember making my way over to the empty desk that had a folded card with my name on it while at least twenty sets of eyes followed me. With my back still turned and before I was fully in my seat, Ms. Hines spoke about me as if I wasn't even there. "I know it seems like it's a little late in the year but Yaminah is a part of our class now. I'm sure it's hard starting at a new school almost at the end of the school year, so make sure you make her feel welcome." She smiled over at me as if to ask if I was ready for something. "Tell us something about yourself, Yaminah. What's something you like to do in your free time?"

That's when I knew Ms. Hines was trying to kill me. She was still across the room, but there was some kind of invisible hand wrapping its fingers around my throat. Every time I opened my mouth to get some air it squeezed harder. Goose bumps multiplied in seconds over every inch of my skin, sweat pooling under my armpits, on my back, and dripping down the backs of my legs, making me hate that my seat was next to the blasting air conditioner. I remember opening my lips just enough to breathe in enough air to not pass out, Ms. Hines shifting in and out of focus. The walls of the room leaning to the left like they were getting ready to fly away. I clenched the sides of my new desk wishing I'd had a seat belt for this spaceship, though I wished I could fly away with the walls, bracing myself for whatever was going to help me in this nightmare. My teeth ground into each other the way they sometimes did when I was asleep for real. I was convinced if I waited long enough to answer, I'd wake up back at my old school, in our old neighborhood, where everyone already knew me. Or in heaven.

Umwhatdollike.Noidiotshesaidwhatdoyouliketodo.Areyoudumb? It'sasimplesimplesimplequestion.Whatdoyoulikeliketodo,Yaminah. Don'tsaysomethingstupid.Don'tmessthisuptheywilllaughlaughlaughatyou. Justsayyouliketohangoutwithyourfriends, I thought. What friends? I had no friends on the north side. I had no family there either. I had to snap out of it. I remember blinking myself back into reality and trying to clear my throat. I'd looked back at Ms. Hines, trying to push the sound of laughter out of my ears, opened my mouth to ask if I could go see the nurse, and started to wheeze.

SIX

The woman behind the counter stands silent, staring at me from behind the fogged glass food covering a few seconds before I realize that she's ready for me to tell her what I want. Manners are a little different in the Caribbean spots in our neighborhood, and she don't have to say nothin' for me to know she's waiting.

I ask for my regular veggie patty wrapped in cocoa bread and a doubles while she finishes packaging Nikki's curry chicken roti with her eyes focused on me. Because Nikki always offers to pay for this, I always order cheap.

"That's all you want, girl? I know you be hungry."

"You right. Let me get a side of plantain, too," I say, knowing damn well—

"We nuh ahv dat," the woman says, almost as if she couldn't wait to tell me no. A large black hairy mole juts out from the edge of her chin, so fat it could have been where the voice came from.

"Then why is it still on the menu?"

"Look, chil', I does say we nuh ahv dat today. We out. Ya want anyting else or wah?" A more-experienced Trini mother waiting in line behind me sucks her teeth loudly near my ear and shuffles back and forth between slippered feet. Over my shoulder, I eyeball her from the overdrawn lip liner down to the length of the tacky magenta muumuu she chose to wear out in public. She shifts her baby higher up on her hip and bucks at me with her eyes. The child clenches the side of her sagging, braless titty, stretched down and across her large belly.

"Oh, you trippin', trippin'," Nikki says, staring at me as if I've forgotten what neighborhood I'm in. "You know they don't never have no plantain left after noon. I don't know who you think you is."

I settle for a bright red premade cup of sorrel from the cooler instead. The woman behind the counter packs my wrapped food into a tiny brown-paper bag, then drops that into a plastic bag. She shuffles over to wait on the next customer before I can even say thank you, shaking her head at the Brooklyn kid who still doesn't get the rules of Brooklyn.

On our way up Utica Ave, we pass by the Popeyes parking lot next to my building, covered in chicken bones and cars that don't even bother to park right. I try to speed up as we cross the street to pass the bodega where Bobby's leaned back against the window with all the blown-up pictures of deli meat and ice cream bars. He takes a big pull of his Newport and nods at me with a lifted eyebrow. His smoke floats just above us, and for a minute, I imagine myself riding the sky till I fade away into nothing.

"That muhfucka stay lurkin'," Nikki says when we're far enough up the block for Bobby not to hear us. "Dudes like him shouldn't be able to work in customer service. Eyes be ready to pop all out anytime somebody with a vagina walk by." We both bust out laughing at the idea that anybody who works in a New York City bodega even thinks about customer service.

It's either they nice to us or they not. But at the end of the day, the people who work in these mini markets all over our neighborhood pretty much follow their own set of rules that don't have nothin' to do with the customer. I learned that quick after we moved here and noticed none of 'em went far to get home. They'd just leave out the door with bells to walk into the door next to it where they live with their families upstairs. The first time we saw Bobby go upstairs to the apartment right above 24/7 Heaven Deli, Pop said we're in their house when we go in there. And that people can do whatever they want in they own house.

———

Nikki Joy lives on the sixth floor of a walk-up a few blocks over from 24/7 Heaven but much farther away from Utica, so it almost feels like we're on a totally different side of Brooklyn. A strong, smoky breeze pumps out the front door of Nikki's apartment along with Ma's and Malachi's voices over the scream-whistle of a teakettle. With her back to us, Ma is setting up her tripod, a ring light, and her yoga mat. Me and Nikki drop our backpacks by the front door, next to the kitchen, walk into the living room, where she stands, and jokingly jump into her shot even though we know she's not recording yet. In the kitchen, Malachi silences the tea whistle, and we hear mugs rattle being pulled from the cupboard.

"It's more to the spotlight than bein' cute, ya know," Ma says, leaning in to kiss each of us on the cheek. "You gotta know how to do somethin' with all that attention. Now move, this space is for facilitators only and I'm gettin' ready to teach. Y'all know the drill," she says, getting all serious before nudging us out of the living-room-turned-online-yoga-studio.

Under the light coming in from all the windows, the spotless hardwood floor shines around Ma's multicolored ankle bracelet and gold toe rings. I quietly take a seat under one of Malachi's paintings at the glass dining table opposite the kitchen, while Nikki pours hot water into two mugs. Malachi takes Ma her cup, gently resting a hand on the small of her back while he kisses her before disappearing into their bedroom with his own.

"I need two of those," I tell Nikki as she drops chamomile tea bags into each of our mugs. I study Ma as if I've never seen her prepare to record one of her classes before. She lights one stick of nag champa, then takes a few deep breaths, pulling her thick tie-dyed yoga pants higher up over the tightest abs I've ever seen on a person. She checks her ass out in the large mirror leaned up against the living room wall. And, listen, it's not something anybody can miss. If it isn't her always-toasty-almond-shea-butter-moisturized skin or the way her long red locs cascade down her back or the way her matching sports bras cup her chest or her melodic singsong voice that could put the most restless of babies to sleep, it's definitely that ass making sure all five thousand of her faithful YouTube subscribers are at attention. She turns on an instrumental that sounds like a mashup of all her favorite soca tracks—a mix she always begins with—and hits record on her phone. Now it's all crossed legs and deep breaths at the edge of her mat. I follow Nikki back to her room, hearing Ma's instructions to "begin in a seated position with both legs crossed, placing your hands wherever your body needs some extra love today . . ."

"Spill it, ho," Nikki immediately demands the second both of us are behind her closed door. Nikki's room is like a portal that only a few privileged plant zaddies, sugar babies, and best friends can enter. Her words, not mine. First, you have to make it through the sheet of beads draped over the door. Then, there's the jungle of plants sitting on various stools and tables situated around the room in a way that only makes sense to Nikki. Even more hang from the ceiling, surrounding the windows that lead out to a fire escape.

"Why I gotta be a ho, though? Why can't I just be the homie?"

"Girl, shut up. You know what I mean. I neeeeed the details. First, you lie to your dad about where you was at the other night. Then, you go the whole school day looking like somebody stole your last pack of cigarettes and then told him about it before you could get some more. Ma says we women"—she air quotes this—"change once we have sex. So, wassup? Have you . . . changed?" Nikki doesn't ever waste time sussing out information that she needs from anybody. Especially me. And she refuses to believe I could go over Mike's house without a little touch-and-feel, as she calls it.

"Sorry to disappoint you, but ain't nothin' to tell. Just went over there to blow off some steam. Get away for a little while. You know Brooklyn be a lot sometimes." She sits across from me on the caramel-colored leather love seat she's got pushed against the wall next to her closet, a gradient rainbow of stage-ready costumes that Nikki wears on a regular day. I unfasten my overalls and let them drop to the floor before sitting down on Nikki's bed. You never sit on somebody's bed with your outside clothes in New York unless you tryna make them cuddle with the houseless people that've rubbed all their bodily juices into the train benches, bus seats, and the general air of this city. With mirrors for sliding doors, I can't help but stare back at myself seated on top of the plush turquoise velvet comforter that's half slid off the edge of her bed.

"So, that's what they callin' it now, huh? You ain't slick."

"I'm serious, nothing really happened."

"Nothing *really* happened, huh? Then what *kinda* happened?" she says, sitting up, placing her elbows on her thighs, and leaning over her knees like she's leading some kind of investigation on who's fucking who.

"I mean we messed around a little and then we stopped. 'Cause Mike was all like 'What's up with you' and I didn't know what he was talkin' 'bout." Nikki pushes some of her curls behind her as if it'd help her hear me more clearly. Or at least expose the lie I'm half telling. I focus my eyes on everything but Nikki's face, where I know I'd crack, fall apart, and disintegrate into dust with just one second of eye contact. Taking in a deep breath of the scents lingering throughout her room—lavender and a hint of peppermint—I look out onto the fire escape, wishing I could be a pigeon for just one day. I'd be able to fly away whenever I wanted to and people would despise me so much, they'd never touch me. No one would ask me about my feelings. People wouldn't even think I had any feelings to ask about at all. And if my mother died, I'd probably see it as nothing more than the circle of life or some shit like that.

"Uh-huh" is all she says back, still staring into me like I'm betraying her but still worthy of a chance. "Come here, girl," she says, sitting back in the seat again and patting the space between her legs. I walk over, turn around, and sit on the floor with my back to her, facing the opposite wall. Nikki pulls the tie holding my hair up on the top of my head to let my twists fall everywhere, combing her fingers through them, gently separating naps that'd begun to cover my parts. She opens the jar of grease that lives permanently on a small table full of succulents beside the love seat. Slowly, she starts rub the grease into my scalp. A large poster of Lizzo's fishnetted ass becomes a small obsession for the few minutes that we sit in silence. The photo is nothing but her hair draping down her lower back and hands holding her own two cheeks. I study the dress, white and hugging ripples of bulging brown skin as if to say, "Here . . . you can kiss it." Around the photo, Nikki's beige walls are covered in affirmations written on yellow Post-its. Nikki hands me a tissue before I even realize I'm crying. Fuck. She moves to another section of my head.

"All right, before I start, can you promise you won't act sorry for me?"

"One thing Nikki Joy ain't is sorry for *any* damn thing. Spill."

"Okay, so like me and Pop had gotten into it. And so, you know, after he left to go gig at Fat Cat, I hit up Mike to kick it at his house. Felt like I couldn't really breathe at my crib, you know?"

"Uh-huh." Nikki hands me another tissue. The tears are streaming down my face and chest before I even get to the part she's waiting for. Or at least the part I know I have to get out.

"So, we get to his crib and soon as he closes the door behind us, I got him against the wall. I'm kissin' his neck. We touchin' and all . . ." I clench my tea mug with both hands, realizing it feels strange as hell to say these details out loud. Even to Nikki. I hadn't really done this before. Mike is my first boyfriend and the first dude I've ever . . . sorta taken it there with. Feels almost like something I'm supposed to keep between me and him, but she's my best friend and I've never kept anything from her for long. I take a deep breath through my belly the way Pop taught me that first time I came home with one of the fevers. "Then, like, I pull him onto the bed and it's getting hot, you know? I start kissing him harder and taking my clothes off and he just starts asking all these stupid questions."

"Like what?" Nikki asks, now combing her fingers through my twists again and pulling them back up into a bun on the top of my head.

"Like . . . what was up with me and why I wanted to do this all of a sudden." Nikki giggles a little but quiets herself immediately, trying not to interrupt me too much before I get to the good parts. "I wasn't expecting that. I thought he'd be happy to finally get what he's been waiting on. I wasn't tryna do all that talkin'. I just wanted to do it."

"Well?" I'm not moving fast enough for Nikki, but she's being as patient as she can. Nikki's good at making me feel safe enough to tell her stuff I wouldn't tell anybody else. And good at pushing me when I'm hesitating on something I should have spit out by now. I take another deep breath.

"I went over Mike's house because I was sad. I thought if I just let him touch me . . . like, really touch me, he'd make me feel better. That he'd make me feel so good that I'd forget everything. Forget everything that I'd just found out earlier in the day." I turn around to face Nikki now. "Sandra is dead. My mama—" I start to cry uncontrollably, and the tears pour without me even trying to clean up the mess. It's okay for me to be a mess here. "No one told me that my mama died, Nikki. That she left for good and that I'll never see her again. She'll never be able to tell me what happened. Why she started being so mean to me. Why everybody was calling her crazy and whispering about her around me. There's so much I don't know about her, Nikki. So much I don't know about me. I just . . . why didn't anybody tell me she was dying? Why did she die? Why did she . . . ?"

The pain chokes me from the inside and a large knot that feels like brass knuckles settles in my throat. Nikki pulls me in hard, my face completely soaking her shoulder. She still doesn't say anything and the room becomes loud with my pitiful sobs.

"How did you find this out, sis?"

I sit back on my feet, open Facebook Messenger, and hand her my phone while I empty my nose in another big wad of tissue.

"Shit. This is terrible. You going?"

"HELL no! Why would I go back there? You know the story. All these years, everybody there's always reminding me that she's my mama and that I only got *one* mama, but what about the fact that I was one of her daughters, huh? Didn't seem like anybody but Pop cared about that when she was cussin' me out and stumbling into the house after a night at the club when she was supposed to be at work. She didn't even try to hide it after a while. No shame or fucks about all the promises she was breaking. "

"Question." Nikki pauses for me to give her a sign that I'm down to answer. I wipe my nose and wait, a silent yes. "Don't you wanna find out all that shit you don't know? Don't you got some people you wanna straighten out?" By straighten out, Nikki means tell them about themselves. Once and for all. Nikki, Pop, and Mike all know I'd sworn off Sandra's side of the family, minus Tiff. Cousin Tiff gets a pass but everybody else? I'm done. I think about what she's asking me right now, and for a second, I fantasize about what it'd be like to cuss Uncle James out. To ask Aunty Jo where she was at when Sandra was gettin' tore up. To look Nana in the face and ask her why she ain't protect me. But my body don't really feel good when I think about all that. All it remembers is the stress of that city. Obsidian: birthplace of my first hurt. I was doing so good far away from them. Without her. Now look at me. Undone over news I thought I wouldn't give a fuck about. News I once thought would feel like every brick falling off my shoulders.

"I don't know. Sounds like drama I don't need."

"Think about it," she says, now leaned back in the seat, licking the edge of an almost perfectly rolled blunt. "In the meantime, come hit this with me."

We climb out her window onto the fire escape. I imagine myself, again, as one of the pigeons that flies off the rail when we go to lean over it, our hands hanging off the edge. I take two puffs and imagine me flying. Out of Brooklyn, past Manhattan. Out of Manhattan and past the Bronx. My wings pumping harder and harder as it leaves the Bronx and flies over Canada into Michigan. Below me, Obsidian sits the same way it has for years: on top of nothing. Gray and lifeless. No longer the place where Sandra Okar lives. Her body now in that ground. I pump my wings harder to circle the city and descend lower to look at the place that's now just a shell of its old self.

Me, wondering what happened to the OB.

How did it just swallow her up like that?

SEVEN

"You not here to propose or nothin' like that, are you? 'Cause
if you are, I'ma need to remind you that I'm way too young for that shit.
And you're wylin' if you think I'm saying yes without Pop's blessing."

The truth is I might mess around and say yes if that's what he's here
to do. Mike looks good as hell standing in our building's front lobby
all nervous and cleaned up. Besides the light pit stains growing under
the arms of his white tee, everything he's wearing looks new and I can
tell his mama finally laid hands on that head of his. With one hand
holding a large brown-paper takeout bag and the other stuffed into his
jeans pants pocket, his jaw tenses a little when he smiles back at me as
I walk past him toward the elevator.

"Chill, chill, chill," he instructs, putting one hand up, flashing all
his pretty teeth. "I brought y'all something." We linger on each side of
the elevator door before I press the button.

"What you mean 'y'all'?"

"You and your pops. Who else?"

"Yo, you sure you not here to propose?" I ask, this time stepping in
close enough to smell the fact that he's got on real cologne. Glancing
down at the bag, I recognize he's brought us something from Peaches,
where both he and Nikki work.

"He here?"

"I mean, yeah, but . . ."

"Can I come up?" Mike's hard to say no to, and though Pop don't really like anybody poppin' up on him, I figure something in that bag could convince him otherwise. I walk over to the elevator and the button lights under the press of my finger. The door opens immediately and Mike steps in behind me. His lips push into mine the minute the door closes back behind us and my body tenses imagining Pop somehow standing there in the hallway of our floor as the door reopens. I gently use my fingertips to push him away. We stand in silence as the small elevator space fills with the funk of foods that smell like they don't go together. I try to investigate the smile that hasn't left his face since I walked through the lobby door.

"Okay, so you hang back for a second while I unlock the door. I don't know what Pop might do if he sees you first," I whisper to Mike, facing him in front of apartment 4J. "And whatever you here to do, it was your idea, okay? I ain't tell you to come over here, and if he asks, I told you to leave."

Pop's shirtless back is to the front door and he immediately starts talking to me the second he hears it close and lock behind Mike. I announce Mike immediately to preserve my own life.

"Pop, he was here before I even got home. I ain't have nothin' to do with it. Love yoooou," I say all in one breath. Mike puts the restaurant bag on the coffee table next to us, the closest table he could reach without taking a step closer to Pop.

"I saw him walk into the lobby from the window 'bout ten minutes ago. I know," he says, now leaned back against the fridge. I make a note for later not to do nothin' suspect in front of the building where he can see from the window. Somehow an apple is in his hand ready for him to bite into just after he says this, and what I thought was about to be a horror scene starts feeling like a dark comedy that don't feel safe to laugh at just yet. The way the loud crunch of the apple cracks the air while Pop holds eye contact with Mike pushes it into parody.

"S-sir, I—I . . . brought y'all somethin' to eat. I got . . ."

"We got food in here, son." Pop gestures to the stove with his eyebrows and says nothing else. The miniature smirk spreading across his face actually looks like a dare. Pop wants Mike to try again. With some bass in his voice. He can smell fear from two boroughs away and Mike's sweaty-ass forehead is standing right here in our apartment, which I still can't believe. Mike clears his throat and lifts his chin up a little, poking his chest out a little bit, too. Go 'head, boo.

"Mr. Okar, I brought you and Yaminah some dinner for tonight." The bass is here. Mike grabs the bag off the coffee table like he's rushing to leave, but opens it and starts walking toward the counter. In the direction of Pop. I squeeze my eyes shut for a second. "For you, I brought our gumbo. Sausage free. I made sure the cooks knew not to put no swine in yours. But it got chicken in it, though. Minah ain't say you was a vegan like her or noth—anything like that." I open my eyes to see him pulling out each dish and describing it to Pop like he was at work or something. But, like, serving a guest in a corner booth reserved only for VIP guests. Okay, boo! I see you.

Pop looks at me as if to ask, *Y'all think y'all slick bringin' me food, huh? I ain't stupid,* and then turns the right burner that was still on under an empty pot of boiling water. I'm one hundred percent sure he wasn't about to do nothin' serious on that stove. My baby is smart.

"And for Minah, we got the vegan margherita pizza. Extra basil," he says to Pop's raised eyebrow. He might be doin' too much.

"Mmm, that smells good, Pop. Almost makes me miss eating pulverized animal flesh." Both of their backs straighten so I can feel the full-on press of their glares.

"Damn, Munch! How am I supposed to enjoy this offering from your little . . . boyfr—friend with you tryna kill my buzz!" Normally he'd pause for us to get his pun but Mike prolly not gonna breathe till he leaves and I've heard all Pop's meat-eater jokes before. I happily raise my hands in surrender.

"My bad. Go 'head, boo," I say before I can catch it. Pop's jaw bounces inside his mouth. Mike moves quick to finish the job.

"Aaaand lastly, I got somethin' botha y'all can get into. This is our gourmet lava cake." Mike, stop. "No dairy, but it's delicious." He starts packing up all the extra napkins, plastic forks, and spoons, and Pop's eyebrows finally look relaxed. "Yeah, so that's it. I hope you like it, Mr. Okar." He heads back to the front door where I'm still standing and turns around. "It was real nice meeting you."

Mike leaves without touching me. I get it. You can't do too much when you want parents on your good side. Pop bites into an extra-large piece of corn bread—that I know Mike hassled the chef for—and takes out a spoon for himself. He removes the lid, and I watch the steam rise off his gumbo. My mouth waters while the smell of his gumbo's Cajun spices mixes with my pizza's nondairy cheez product. He starts to slurp right from the pint-sized Styrofoam to-go bowl without a word, unless you count the way black people hum and dance a little when the food's good. I don't tell Pop I wish his food was mine and he doesn't pull out a plate for me. Ain't no unnecessary dishes getting made in this house and he knows I'll be inhaling this pizza straight out the box from the safety of my bed.

"Tell your lil boyfriend he can come back on Friday for some real food," he says.

EIGHT

Probably for the first time ever, I notice somebody's cut the grass. And I ain't ever think too much about the bushes before, but they look so perfect I almost believe they're fake. To be honest, plastic bushes planted in an apartment building's front lawn wouldn't be that surprising in Crown Heights. It's pretty normal for some of these Caribbean grandmas to keep pots of tacky fabric flowers outside year-round on the more residential streets. The streets with actual houses, yards, and sometimes, a little spot to park a car if you gully enough to drive in New York. Where me and Pop live is sort of the opposite of all that, though. Pop don't have a car and Nikki calls our apartment the hood building 'cause of all the drama that goes on just outside of it. It's a seven-story rectangular brick building that looks like it's been set on fire a few times but was too corroded with the Brooklyn grind for the outside world to penetrate. Nikki talks a lot of shit about the occasional piss smell looming in the staircase when the elevator breaks down, but she ain't never complained about being able to smoke a blunt in there without anybody calling the police. Our building looks like it'd swing first if somebody tried to run up. And we got people like Old Man if they do. People like Old Man see everything.

"If you don't take that silly-ass tie off before we get up there, I'ma act like I never met you, fam. You'd seriously be on your own," Nikki tells Mike while we watch the elevator door close behind us. She talks to every dude like just their being alive exhausts her, even though Mike mostly gets a pass. Mike presses the number four in slow motion while keeping eye contact with me. He thinks he already in there with Pop but he don't know that little intro was only round one. If he walks in our apartment like this, the way he is now, Pop will surely let off at least two more rounds of Dad ammo and Mike really don't want those problems. "For real, that white button-down and black tie they gave you *for work* is too much. We're just having dinner with Minah's dad. We not finna be at no opera," she pushes.

"Yo, you talk like you actually been to an opera, knowing yo ass ain't never been to nothing like that," Mike snaps back. It's true. Though Nikki always says she's tryna help prepare me for the world, she's never even been out of New York State. Not even once. Obsidian ain't really nothin' to talk about, but at least me and Pop chose to come here. Nikki was born and raised in Brooklyn. Everything she thinks about the world she learned from the internet, including the hours of time she spends studying Lizzo and Kendra Austin for style inspiration. I reach for Mike's collar.

"Nikki got a point, babe," I say, lifting up the starched collar of his button-up and loosening the knot just under his neck. "Pop is a whole professional and ain't never worn a suit in his life. He's not gon' be impressed. He's gonna think you're tryna cover something up." Mike pulls off his fitted, revealing cornrows still fresh from the other day and I lift the tie loop off his neck and over his head. A light whiff of coconut and lime comes off his freshly greased scalp. His fingers move as fast as a West African braider in Harlem, unbuttoning his shirt as the elevator beeps to pass the third floor. I slide it off his back just as the floor jerks, settles, and the doors part to let us off at the fourth.

"If I didn't know this scrub personally, I might have thought that lil scene was kind of cute," Nikki says, stomping in front of us toward 4J. Today the boots are giving intergalactic combat and we are mere earthlings following her lead into the unknown of Pop's suspicious invitation. She pauses in front of the door and waits silently for Mike to get himself all the way together, using wide, glitter-coated eyelids to rush us. I toss Nikki his work shirt. She catches it and stuffs it into her backpack all in one move. I want to thank baby Jesus, Allah, Oshun, and everybody else who up in the sky who might have been responsible for Mike's undershirt looking brand-fresh-from-the-Hanes-pack-new. With it slightly tucked in, and his fitted kept in his hand, he almost looks like somebody Pop could trust his daughter with, if anybody like that exists. Nikki is only able to get one knock in before we hear all three locks being unlatched from inside.

Our apartment didn't come with enough space for a dining table or nothin' like that, so all four of us sit on the floor around the coffee table on some hippie shit. The fact that Pop ordered Chinese food from our favorite spot in Bed-Stuy means he wants peace. It's the only takeout we can agree on 'cause we don't gotta share and he can eat all the charred chicken flesh he wants. But sitting around a table having dinner with my dad, my boyfriend, and my best friend makes me forget that I'm even hungry. It feels too good to be true. The first five minutes of this felt like the longest five minutes of my life, watching eight hands dodging and clashing against one another as we reached for a whole spread of rice, spring rolls, and a bunch of meats coated in red and brown sauces. And if I could handle the sound of everybody chewing in silence, I wouldn't have been the first person to speak.

"Pop, you know how to poach an egg?"

"Fuck is 'poach'?"

Guess not.

"And you say you a vegan," Nikki says. "I knew you been dreamin' about yolk this whole time, gworl. Come back on this side."

"It's what you do to a egg that you want to bust all on top of your food," I inform the table, proudly.

Mike chokes on the spring roll he'd just tried to inhale before letting it cool off enough. Oil drizzles down the side of his mouth and he opens his mouth loudly, tryna release hot air instead of letting it drop out of his mouth back onto the plate like I would have. I know Nikki's resisting the urge to debut a perfectly timed sex joke in front of Pop. This is going so well.

"Yeah, yeah, like on eggs Benedict or—or like . . . on top of some crispy-ahh—crispy home fries," Mike adds. Watching him and Nikki try to be respectful by not cussin' in front of somebody who just said "fuck" is pure comedy.

"So, you askin' me if I know how to put a raw egg on my food . . . to eat? I'm good off that, Munch," Pop says, using his hands to throw back a large piece of fried egg he'd fished out of his beef-fried rice with his fingers.

"Yeah, *hard* pass," Nikki says, reaching around the large bouquet of flowers she brought to grab another packet of duck sauce. It's obvious the large vase full of lilies, sunflowers, and roses, dressed up with other useless flowers I don't know the names of, doesn't match the food, the occasion, or our apartment, but they're a beautiful distraction. Mike and I had set the table in a rush as if food would make Pop forget a boy his daughter had spent the night with was in his house. Nikki tells him all "family" dinners need flowers at the center of the table, as she tries to sneak a wink in my direction. I catch it and force my eyes back down where I can focus on safer things like chopsticks, napkins, and the plastic bags the food came out of with the words *thank you* printed three times in bold red lettering on the side.

"Well, unlike y'all uncultured black people"—I pause to make it clear I'm talking to Pop and Nikki only—"I know how to do it. Kofi taught us." The fact that my yolk broke into a million pieces in my pot during home-ec class isn't relevant.

Sandra had taught Pop how to make the perfect fried egg. I wasn't there for it, but one time Pop caught himself showing me how to fry an egg the Sandra Way when we first moved into the apartment one Saturday morning. Butter. Then the egg. Then salt. Then black pepper. A pinch of cayenne pepper. Gently fold it in half once the clear egg white really turns white. The yolk runs all over your food that way, too. I hadn't known it was actually her recipe until that day 'cause Pop was always the one to make us breakfast back in the OB. Breakfast time was when Sandra got back from the night shift and we only had a few minutes to talk before it was time to go to school. The dark circles under her eyes and drunken delirium of an overnight shift never stopped her from trying to catch up with me before I had to get outside to catch the school bus.

Sandra never used to go anywhere before without letting me know she'd be back. Even when she'd step outside each morning for a cigarette while Pop made them breakfast, she'd always say, "See you later, Minah Baby. Mama's just gonna go take a walk. I wanna hear all about what you did in school yesterday when I'm back, okay?" Grown folks are always calling smoking cigarettes "taking a walk," as if I couldn't see the smoke coming from around the side of our apartment building, floating up into our windows. As if I couldn't always smell the stench coming off every pair of the scrubs she wore to work each night. She'd rush into the house and drop her work bag next to where I sat scarfing down my Frosted Flakes. She'd bend down to kiss me on the cheek and then disappear around the corner of our apartment building for the five minutes it took me to finish eating. She'd come back looking just as tired but happy, sitting across from me with one leg relaxed over the other. "Tell me everything, girl," she'd say, studying me and sipping from her mug as if waiting for the latest elementary school gossip. Mama always treated our quiet morning time like girl talk even if Pop was just a few feet away. We'd laugh like best friends and she'd even let me take a few sips of her coffee. I'd leave the shimmery purple lipstick mark on my cheek all day for every teacher to see.

"So what should we do about my dead mom, y'all?" I ask, reaching for the General Tso's tofu. All the loud chewing stops and I hear a long gulp move down Mike's throat. I put the plastic container down after my second scoop and reach for the pint of rice closest to me. I don't look up until I've shoveled half of it onto my plate. "All this food and y'all just gon' stop eating?" I laugh. "Couldn't be me!" Hard. But only for a few minutes. I scoop a heap of rice onto my spoon with a small piece of tofu, put it in my mouth, and close my eyes. Sandra always closed her eyes when food was good. That's how you make something that feels good last for a long time: by closing your eyes and forgetting anything else exists until you believe it'll last forever.

"Minah, maybe we should—" Pop starts.

"Maybe we should what? Pretend? I've had enough of that, John," I snap, biting into a spring roll. I feel Nikki's breath stop a bit. Mike leans back in his seat and braces himself for whatever comes after a black child calls their whole-ass daddy by his first name. It's not something they've ever seen or would ever do. Both of them are Caribbean and would never try no American shit like that, lest they continue the rest of their lives in a grave. But my mama is in the grave, so fuck it.

Pop drops his head into his hands over his plate and lets out a long, exhausted sigh that sounds like the breath Nikki's mom is always calling Ujjayi. Imagine the sound of somebody lettin' they breath out like they don't want it all to come out at once. That. Nikki catches her breath and leans in.

"You okay, sis—"

"I'm not." What a stupid question. "Would you be? What am I supposed do now, huh? If I go, everybody gon' be bringing her up and shit and talking about her like she was some typa angel. They gon' be asking me why I don't come around no more and making a big deal about how tall I've grown like they had something to do with it. If I don't go, they gon' keep talkin' behind my back about how I think I'm so much better than everybody just because I left. And Fatimah will be the main one leading it all." Everyone is silent, pushing rice around our plates, eyes focused down on the table. Pop lifts his head and sits his chin on top of clasped hands.

"I know it seems like everybody was tryna keep something from you, Munch. And I'm sorry about that." He pauses to take another deep breath. "I want you to know I support whatever you decide to do. You don't have to go if you don't want to. And if you want to, I'll buy your plane ticket tomorrow." Tomorrow. Tomorrow is too close to today and Pop don't have extra money lying around like that for me to be saying yes to plane tickets if I might change my mind.

"Remember that time you told me you miss your old house back in Obsidian? How you said, sometimes, the houses down the street remind you of the ones in your granny's hood?" Mike asks. My neck almost snaps the way my body jerks, suddenly remembering he's even here. I don't know where he's going with this but I catch a glimpse of the surprised look on Pop's face and wonder.

"Yeah."

"You couldn't see your face that day. I mean, you can't ever really see your own face unless you in the mirror. But, you just looked so happy when you said it. I know I haven't known you as long as your pop and all, but maybe that feeling you have when you think about y'all's old house is worth going back for." I notice Pop's shoulders drop out the corner of my eye. "I mean, Brooklyn is cool and all, but maybe Obsidian won't be as bad as you remember it."

Maybe, just like me, it's changed.

Won't none of the doctors know how to catch it or what it is they tryna catch before it eats you up, fast. The youngins gon' be too young to realize it's death that they see comin', so at first the grown folks will lie. They'll see the glass twistin' us all kinds of ways and tell them we needed to stay longer at the place they last saw us goin'. That we'll just be away for a little while so we can get better. Or that we've gone to see somebody that needs our help. Or that it just didn't work out. Problem is little girls start hating us if they stop seeing us because we gone too much. We always gone. But when they get to high school, and grown folks start to figure they old enough to know we ain't comin' back, the grown folks lie some more. Say we ate somethin' bad. Say we was just laughing one day at another one of our silly jokes that turned into a cough and that cough turned into a bellyache so bad it stopped us from breathin'. The day we just couldn't stop coughin' after the joke was over and the blood wouldn't stop splashing from our mouths into our hands, they'll take us away while our little girls are in school. But the little girls will catch them packing. Will notice our suitcase gone when they get back and wonder. Never mind the fact that won't be no suitcases needed where we've gone now.

HIS

ONE
MONTH
LATER

NINE

I don't care what anybody says, I'm not giving a damn thing back to the hood. And by "the hood," I mean Obsidian, Michigan.

People always talkin' 'bout the American dream but it feels like it's two of those, you know? In the first type, the one everybody means when they say it, you get good grades, go off to a nice college, get a fancy job, make grown-folks money, get married to the love of your life, buy a big house with a fence and a yard, have mad kids . . . shit like that. But the other one, the one for the poor black people, the dream is to leave. The dream is to get the fuck out of the place you came from so you can have a life better than the one you had growing up. The one where your parents sacrificed every joy, every penny, their everything so you could have what they didn't. But it don't stop there. Not only do they expect us to get up out of here. They expect us to come back and share whatever we got out in the world with the place we came from so that somebody else like us can have a chance, too. But who wants to throw money into a dump where don't nobody ever see anything good come of it? Who wants to put their hand in a garbage disposal? Who wants to go back to a place where don't nobody live in a house that even comes with one of those, huh? Who wants to throw all their hard work into the trash, a place that don't do nothing but chew you up and spit you out into a landfill, the place where things that were once good go to die? Obsidian, birthplace of Yaminah Okar. Origin of all my first heartbreaks and the last city I wanna be in right now. I told myself I was done with this place, but here I am.

"Biiiitch, tell me why Kobe and Maleek was showin' they whole ass on Nana's front lawn yesterday? Like, legit throwin' hands in front of her house where err'body could see our business? Can't take they asses nowhere. Even to they own granny house," Tiffany says, shaking her head while lifting one of my bags into her popped trunk. She never misses a beat and laughs at this family gossip like she's telling me Deacon Isaac slept with another one of the choir directors at the church our family goes to—the one everyone at least puts their good clothes on for to attend Easter service. Tiff always laughs like it ain't something we should be ashamed of.

"Oh, word?" I say, unenthused and faking interest at something that's hardly new. Nothing's changed, of course. I steady my umbrella over her head while tossing my backpack in before she closes it.

"Yeah, girl, they was scrappin' for real. One minute they playin' cards out on the front porch, the next tables is flippin', cups flyin', words is being exchanged, and bows is being thrown! Shit was better than WWE."

I disagree without having been there to see it myself. "Have you ever, in your life, even watched wrestling before?"

"Nope, but I know that they be fighting on there," she says, making a fist and rolling it toward her own face to make faux black eyes. She unlocks the doors to her Honda. A soccer-mom car for sure, but a nicer soccer-mom car than Sandra ever had. We laugh at the fact that we know neither of us has seen a single WWE match and the laughter dies off with us shaking our heads at the shame of my cousins doing what we expect them to do. All day, every day. "And you know Kobe won."

The rain beats down on Tiff's roof like Kobe's fists against Maleek's head any given day when there wasn't much to do in Obsidian. And there's never really anything good to get into in the OB anymore. Through the downpour I watch the Six Lane Bowl move quick past my window on the way to Nana's house, the stale stench of feet filling my nose at my first memory there. We always used the lane with the gutter guards to make me feel good, throwing the orange five-pound ball down the lane with both my tiny hands. I look to the left past Tiff to see the Family Films zoom past us, all the lights out and a rusted CLOSED sign looming over a sad parking lot that ain't had cars parked in it for years.

Tiff pulls into the Kroger grocery a few blocks down and tells me to chill while she runs in for a few things real quick before asking me if I want anything.

"Nah, I'm good."

"Cool, 'cause it's Thursday and payday is Friday. I was just bein' nice, Cuz," she says with a smirk. With that she slams the car door shut, sending it into a long shake that Tiff is completely unfazed by. I cut the radio on and it's already set to 97.9. Before letting my seat all the way back to close my eyes for a second, I make sure all the doors are locked and turn up the volume to muffle the depressing sounds of the nothing happening around me. I wake to a tapping on my window and almost jump out of my skin when I see it ain't Tiff . . . or anybody else that would be allowed to be this close to her car. The old man taps the window again, almost like he's annoyed, seeing me rub my eyes back into this day and time.

"Yes?" I say through the window, already irritated. There's a reason why I made sure all the doors were locked before I let my guard down. He wobbles a bit before lifting and shaking a dingy paper cup that clinks with maybe three or four pennies in front of me. "Naw, I don't have nothin, sorry." I look away to start lowering myself back and he taps again. This time harder. "I said I don't have nothin' for you, G! Go 'head!" The amount of hair growing from most of the old man's face makes it hard to see his facial expression but the way he shuffles away tells me he believed I was lying. That I must have something in my pockets to give him since he don't usually see anybody that looks like me around here. Figures. Don't nobody around here look they been anywhere else. And I'm a New Yorker now. I'm not to be confused with the people who weren't smart enough to get up out of this dead end. Just as I start dozing again, another loud tap at the door. This time on Tiff's side, and I exhale, relieved to see it's actually her this time.

"I'm glad you gettin' sleep now," she says, sliding into her seat after I unlock her door. "'Cause you not finna get none for the rest of your trip." Tiff throws two grocery bags full of chips over into the back seat and shines teeth that look like a mouthful of pearls drenched in Vaseline. For a long time, me and my other cousins had bets that she'd never lost a tooth like the rest of us when we were kids. It couldn't be possible that she'd lost any the way her mouth always seemed packed with teeth that looked too small for her age. And while the rest of us were pressed to spend our tooth-fairy money on penny candy from Nana's cart, she was flashing five- and ten-dollar bills. Convinced the tooth fairy wasn't unfair enough to be dishing that kind of money to only one of us, we finally got Tiff to admit that she was getting an allowance, something none of our parents could afford. Luckily, she was smart and started splitting it with all of us to avoid getting jumped for thinkin' she's better than somebody.

"Please, everything around here be closed by nine o'clock," I say with a shrug. "We 'bout to turn up at Nana's?"

"Uh, yeah, actually," Tiff replies matter-of-fact. "Nana's chill. We don't bother her; she don't mess with us. You'd know that if you came around sometimes. She's different than when we was kids, you'll see. But I'm not even mad, girl. I know you on to bigger and better things. I'm next." I know Tiff enough to know her comments weren't meant to be a burn, but a fact. I'm never here. On purpose.

We pass more businesses in silence, and even though it's Sunday, I'm confused by how many are closed. Five minutes more into the drive the CLOSED signs start turning into large white FOR SALE signs with phone numbers people can call if they're interested in turning what we used to know into what other people think it could be. I don't pay too much attention to what street we're on 'cause I never really had to when we lived here. I still don't know how to drive 'cause ain't no need to drive in Brooklyn. But something still feels strange. We turn a corner where I expect to see a busy Chuck E. Cheese parking lot with families going in and kids coming out. I expect to see dirty, sugar-drunk second graders climbing into minivans, bellies full of cheap pizza and likely smelling of piss after spending too much time in the infamous ball pit. But none of that was there. Instead, we drive past an empty parking lot next to a sad-looking beige-colored office building.

"Where we going?"

"To Nana's, where else?" Tiff says, confused by what sounds like a stupid question. I mean, it should be obvious where we're going 'cause that's where I always stay. But I don't recognize none of this shit that I'm seeing. Where I expect the sidewalks to turn into a wide, tree-lined streets with nothing but houses, parks and picnic spaces built for family cookouts, everything has become freshly paved cement sidewalks or new condos in progress, complete with construction tape and signs for people to keep out.

"Are you sure? This don't look like Nana's neighborhood at all," I say.

"Yeah, girl. They got a whole city plan they been rolling out for years. The west side really startin' to look like downtown," she explains. "I'm not even mad, though. Black folks need jobs and ain't nobody finna find work surrounded by abandoned houses."

"But people used to live here."

"*Live* is a strong word, cuz," she says, turning the corner down another street I don't recognize. "Nana say all those people was just passing through. Same way she say we all just passin' through. What do people who look like us really own in this country, anyway?" she says, throwing up one hand and pausing, then continuing as if responding to her own question. "That's why all I worry about is getting' mines and living to the fullest." A feeling of relief starts washing over me at the sight of a street sign that says BLACKMON DRIVE. Tiff makes a left turn and I'm slightly comforted seeing less random businesses and more houses, but that feeling leaves just as quickly as it came. Much of the houses' insides were on the outside. Literally. Lawns covered in old mattresses, tipped-over cardboard boxes half-full with stuffed animals, old stoves that look like they'd started and been caught in fires, torn-open trash bags filled with left-behind clothes—all of it covered in dirt and surrounding abandoned houses where people we used to know once lived. Tiff makes a right turn at a stop sign on a street marked KILLIGANS STREET. Nana's street. More trees begin to appear, along with houses that still got life in them and so do the people. Hella people on a hot Friday in July. Tiff pulls into the driveway, and suddenly I want to go home. Brooklyn, home.

Tiff cuts the ignition, and I feel my body slump deeper into the leather passenger seat, the backs of my thighs beginning to stick and burn. Tiff takes a long look at herself in the rearview mirror. As she applies another thick coating of lip gloss, I study the side of her face instead of getting out the car. She mostly has the same face as she did when we were kids except now she's even more concerned about her appearance. Tiffany's always been skinny and black as an Obsidian night sky with no stars in it. Kids in the neighborhood used to call her OB's baby 'cause she's so black, and it made her obsess over her looks way more than necessary. At five eleven with measurements like a life-sized Barbie, I could see her on a New York Fashion Week runway if she wasn't so awkward about her height and if she could part with her weave. The struggle ponytail with barely enough hair to pull into it has now graduated into a long, wet-and-wavy wig she now pulls on top of a stocking cap every morning. She forms her mouth into duck lips at her reflection before spritzing herself with body spray that stings the back of my nose. I cough.

"You know you don't gotta wait for me to get out the car. Kobe right there on the porch. He gon' get your bags, boo. Go say hi to somebody or something," she commands, nudging me with her elbow.

"Yo, who are you getting' all cute for? Kobe ain't nobody."

She laughs and adjusts the built-in bra of her pink tank top, making sure her titties are sitting proper but also covered up enough so Nana don't fuss about her lookin' fast. I push the door open and drag myself out the car. It takes Kobe all of five long steps to make it to my side of the car, and before I can stop him, he's scooped me up into his arms, squeezing me so hard I almost can't breathe. "Put me down, I ain't no lil baby!" I scream through a laugh I can't help. Kobe's mostly known for being quick to throw hands but all of us know he's a big-ass, cuddly teddy bear who fights 'cause his heart is too big. The hands usually get thrown 'cause somebody tried to mess with family. Or if you're his brother. He finally lets my feet touch the ground again and steps back to size me up.

"Damn, c-c-cuz, look at you. M-m-muhfuckas leave for a couple years and come back lookin' like money. I s-s-s-s-see you!" Kobe always looks like he just finished fixing somebody's car. Patches of sweat stain an old blue Superman T-shirt he refuses to give up. Standing at five five, he's been the same height since he was eleven. Only difference is he's got a little more muscle and the shirt Uncle James gave him back when he started getting bullied at school fits tighter around his biceps and shoulders, the neckline a little loose from wearing it multiple times a week. "Let me get my shit together before you start b-b-bein' embarrassed to be seen with me in public," he jokes, smiling. He moves the brim of his fitted from the back to the front and reaches out to graze one of my twists. "Granny ain't even tell me you was comin'. How long you gon' be here?"

TEN

Nana's kitchen is everything all at once, just like I remember.
It's a clusterfuck of smells, sounds, and sticky feelings, and you wouldn't
be able to tell how big it is 'cause of all the stuff she's managed to fit in
it. This old house wears hella hats.

Today, Nana's kitchen is beauty salon, community pantry, and
nursery. She almost doesn't catch my face when Tiff announces me
to her. When we walk in, she's standing near the counter, closest to the
sink, with her back to the entrance of the kitchen. Her elbows move
quickly up and down, and I know there's a child sitting in the chair in
front of her getting their scalp pulled clean off the skull by the sound
of the small whimpers. No doubt that baby's been popped at least
three times by now for making any noise at all. Nana never believed
in nobody being tender-headed. She turns, immediately releasing a
squeal-gasp, letting a fistful of taut hair loose, and screams.

"LOOK AT MY BABYYYYYYY!" She limps to my side of the
kitchen, expertly dodging multiple boxes of canned SpaghettiOs;
a stroller; about five toy cars; a headless Cabbage Patch doll; a giant,
unopened box of Avon products; and past a dining table covered in
industrial-sized cleaning supplies to hug me. Nana reeks of pink oil
moisturizer and Eco Style hair gel, like doing hair is her job for real.
I inhale deep while my face is still pressed into her neck and pick up
stale hints of fried sausage and Chanel No. 5. Nana wakes way before

everybody so she's had a whole-ass day already. She pulls me from her chest, plants an uncomfortably wet kiss on my cheek, and gasps again. "Wow! Let Granny get a good look atchu. Still ain't that tall yet . . . you've taken after ya mama. And I see you still runnin' round here dressed like a lil boy!"

Just like it did Sandra, my lack of femininity annoys Nana. But if I was walking around here dressed like Tiff, she'd still have somethin' slick to say. To Sandra and Nana, "like a lil boy" really only means I'm not obsessed with makeup, booty shorts, and miniskirts like the other girls around here.

"Hi, Nana . . ." She turns me all the way around like a chicken in a rotisserie. I feel almost tender enough to fall off the bone, being here in her arms. Almost forget the chaos I'm in until the child in the faux salon chair starts crying. I realize I have no idea who the child is. And in Nana's house, the child could be anyone. I look around Nana's shoulder to see Tiff's taken Nana's spot behind the chair, pulling parted sections of greasy hair tightly into a multicolor bobos. I'm 100 percent sure there will be bumps all over that baby's forehead after she's done. "Nana, who is that?"

"You been gone so damn long, Minah," she says, shaking her head as if the question made her unbearably tired. "That's Robyn, Fatimah's baby." What? Before I can respond, Maleek walks in the kitchen looking like he just came from the gym. But instead of dumbbells, the veins bulging from his forearms are caused by the ridiculous number of grocery bags he's got in each hand.

"Who is—" he starts to ask, peeping it's a girl he thinks he's never seen before in Nana's house, until I turn around.

"MINAH! Sheeeit, what up, CUZ! Damn, man, what you doin' here?" Does anybody in this family actually talk to each other? He drops all the bags and slaps hands with me like one of his homies around the way. The slap turns into a shake and he pulls me. The summer musk of sweat and grape Swishers is familiar. For a second, I relax in his arms until I realize Maleek's hair is longer than mine. I grab a handful and lift it in the air like it stinks. Naturally buffer than Kobe, he looks sorta like Marshawn Lynch, if you squint.

"You think you cute or somethin'?" Maleek blushes like he don't have to beat every girl on the block off with a stick. Him and Kobe don't fight for no reason. Maleek always been the one with the so-called looks and Kobe was only blessed with hard hands and quick feet. Maleek gets the girls and Kobe only gets warnings, even though Kobe ain't fighting by himself. Last time I saw him he only had little nubs all over his head and now he's got major hangtime. He even got a little saucy and dyed the tips orange. He grazes his extra-long goatee and ruffles my ponytail.

"Ahhhh, I do a lil somethin' from time to time," he says, cheesing, obviously too full of himself. "Wassup with you, though? Whatchu doin' here?"

Am I not family? Is the reunion not this weekend?

"I—" Fatimah storms into the kitchen sweaty and flushed, her body bulging from different parts of her outfit as she drops a large cardboard Aldi box full of food at her feet. Head to toe she looks like she's dressed for three different seasons on purpose. From her outdated bedazzled off-the-shoulder Baby Phat T-shirt to the ripped stretch skinny jeans to the stained and leaning Uggs to the fact that it all fits like it's two sizes too small, you can only tell we're sisters in the face. And I know Fatimah hates that every day she has to look in the mirror and see my face.

"Yaminah comes to town and EVERYBODY stops in they tracks,

huh? Forget the ones who BEEN here," she cuts, immediately annoyed with me and Maleek being in conversation. This is the closest to a hello that I'ma get. "It's still bags in the truck, Maleek, damn! You said you would be right back."

Nana limps back over to where Robyn still sits, hiccups from all the crying, jerking her body between quiet sobs. Tiff switches places with Nana again and hands her the rest of the barrettes so she can finish the job.

"AND GIVE ME MY DAMN BABY!" Fatimah demands.

"Chil', I know you mad but you in *my* house and if it wasn't for me, your *damn* baby would still be walkin' around here looking busted and baldheaded, so lower your voice talkin' to me," Nana snaps firm, yet still not raising her voice. She adjusts her blond wig and pats her pocket for her pack of cigarettes after the last barrette is in place. Robyn starts to follow Fatimah out the kitchen.

"What do you say, Robyn?" Nana says more like a command, than a question.

"Tane tou," she says bashfully, pausing and turning around. She looks like us.

"You welcome, baby," Nana says, following Robyn and Fatimah out the kitchen for a smoke. "Welcome home, Minah."

They leave me with the echoes of what being back here sounds like. Tiff follows them all back out the door.

ELEVEN

The basement is an entirely different world from the one upstairs. Sort of.

If you think about all the stuff she got goin' on up there, this ain't that far from it, except it's the after-dark version. The version of Nana's world that comes alive when she's knocked out under a cocktail of cigarettes, Benadryl, and high-blood-pressure pills two floors above us. It ain't no different 'cause, just like upstairs, downstairs operates like a whole bunch of hustles at once. Her house is old, and she's always telling somebody how they don't build houses like hers no more, and that's why the white folks is callin' her phone every day offering to take it off her hands for cold hard cash, as they call it. She's been using every corner of this house for everything she can think of under the sun to make sure she keep the lights on and her babies fed. Babies like us who she says need to be looked out for or the world will eat us up and call us junk food. Me, Tiff, Kobe, and Maleek sit around a small, ash-covered glass table on couches probably older than all of us put together with four rooms pressing on our backs.

The first room you see just at the bottom of the stairs is a dingy laundry room that doubles as a sewing room and mini shoe-repair shop. But I don't know how anyone could do anything in that room for more than five minutes with the sour smell of clothes that's been damp for too long coming from it. Room number two has an old seventies-style barber chair and a large supply cabinet full of snacks and candy to sell from a cart Nana keeps near the front door. The cabinet is locked so none of us steal any. But all of us have stolen from it. Me and Fatimah were nine when Kobe found a way to pick the cheap lock with a hanger from Nana's closet two days after her speech about not touching her "business supplies." We've been dipping into her neighborhood hustle ever since. The third room is a fully equipped music studio, walls patched up with soundproof foam and decorated with a growing collection of cheap lava lamps. Opposite the keyboard, speakers, and a small microphone booth are three desktop computers that somehow still work, even though they look plucked from the early 2000s. The fourth room, always closed with colorful letters strung across the door on a flimsy piece of string, was the nursery. But all Nana's babies, as she calls the toddlers everybody on the block trusts her with, all end up outside. Tiff was a block baby.

"I already know. It's gon' be a hot mess," Tiff says, trying to hold the smoke in her mouth long enough to feel it. "You think everybody gon' come . . . I mean, like, with everything that happened last time?" She asks all of us, exhaling as a thick cloud pours out of her nose and mouth, surrounding her head.

"Don't look at me. I wasn't here," I say, taking the blunt from her hand, a few of her long, sharp acrylic nails scraping a finger. Girly shit makes no practical sense. But neither does this family. Even though I wasn't here, I can imagine all the shit that happened 'cause it's been happening our whole lives. I notice Kobe staring at the side of my face out the corner of my eye. "Fuck you lookin' at? I'm grown."

"Since when do you s-s-smoke, Minah?" he asks, more serious than I feel like dealing with. Kobe always acting like somebody's daddy. He was this way even when we were kids. He was the one that warned us about the headache we'd have the morning after we stole sips from Nana's liquor cabinet. He was the one that went off on Fatimah the day she dared me to smoke my first cigarette in front of all her friends and laughed while they watched me choke. He was always the one fighting something for us, even though none of us paid him any mind given the fact he couldn't seem to keep himself out of trouble. How could he even talk? His warnings came from experience. He's older than me and Tiff, but Father's name is John, not Kobe. I don't answer him. He smirks and nods his head. "Cool, you go away and come back actin' all s-suddity but you obviously still one of us." I exhale heavy whiteness in his direction and ignore his comment, passing to Maleek.

"Chill, she just got here and you already on one."

"I'm cool, 'Leek." Kobe doesn't take his eyes off me. All of us know to back off when he says he's cool. All of us know his insides are always boiling and that he's far from cool. He makes me wonder what it's like to always be on edge like that. What it's like to care so much for a family that's always labeling him "bad" instead of "protective." "Hotheaded" instead of "frustrated with all this stuff he's gotta deal with around here." I don't wanna know what that's like. What it's like for me is enough. When I sit here in this basement with my cousins, all the good memories from when we were kids start rushing back. I feel some good feelings in my heart, but this ain't home no more. It just can't be.

"You live in muhfuckin' New York. What you been gettin' into, my G? I see you. Walkin' in here lookin' like a celebrity. Big City Minah." I hear Maleek say this in a way that makes me wonder if he's being sarcastic or really wants to know what my life's been like all these years since the last family reunion I showed up for back in 2014. I'd felt my phone buzz repeatedly in my pocket just as he'd started talking.

When I take it out, I see a bunch of texts from Mike and a few from Pop and start texting back as fast as I can. Being here swept me up so fast I forgot to tell them I made it safe and, honestly, it feels good to be reminded I live hundreds of miles from here. There's people who love me somewhere else who are worried about me. I was careful about how I unlocked the screen to respond to Mike without anybody getting in my business or accusing me of acting like I'm too important not to be in my phone right now. But I don't realize I'm cheesing hard into the phone the way I always do when it's Mike on the other end. The way I do when I've forgotten where I am.

"Looks like Big City Minah got her a lil boo," Tiff says, speaking for the group.

"What? Nah, shut up" is all I can push out. I've never been good at pretending.

"What's his name?" Tiff pushes.

"Dude prolly n-n-named Chico!" Kobe screams. Tiff and Maleek laugh so hard that Tiff leans over and falls into my shoulder while Maleek bends over his knees wiping tears, trying to catch his breath.

"Oh, nah, that muhfucka p-prolly named Alonzo, or s-somethin' like that, AHAAAAAAAAAAA"! Now Maleek's up grabbing his side like he got a cramp and fake jogging around the room, running into walks, upping the dramatics even more. "Dude prolly wild hell. He w-w-wear Timbs all year, don't he, Minah? Tatts all on his face like that one light-skinned dude with rainbow hair who snitched on all his p-p-people . . . what's that dude name?" He pauses in place, snapping his fingers.

"Don't matter what his name is. He got lil Minah cheesing all up in her phone screen like we n-n-not here." Kobe sits up and leans forward, and I look up. "Yo daddy know you out here thinkin' you grown wit' Dominican m-muhfuckas named Alonzo?"

I sit up and lean forward, too. "You think I'm dumb enough to tell you my business even if I was? Pop wanted to make sure I made it safe and he was gettin' worried that I ain't text him yet. I thought it was funny. Any more information you think I owe you?"

He smirks and traces his faint mustache and down the sides of his mouth. He looks over at Maleek, who's now back in his seat twisting the grinder.

"What y'all been out here doing in Obsidian? Y'all's mama know you be in the streets?"

Maleek looks back at Kobe as if they're having a whole conversation telepathically.

"M-m-my mama and the rest of the grown folks around here don't have time to know nothin' about what's going on in real life. Mama so busy pretending to love Jesus she don't even ask. And if b-by in the streets you mean handling my business so I can take care of me and mine, I hope everybody know. I hope they know when I see stuff g-going down around here, I do something. I don't just leave. I do what I gotta do." Kobe's stutter always sort of disappears for a little bit when he's more than serious. It's always been that way and every time I get scared.

"Aight, Barack, thank you for being the change," Tiff says, cough-laughing with a hand on her chest. "Went down the wrong pipe," she says, waving the smoke from around her face as if that's gonna do anything about her lightweight lungs.

"Keep talkin," Kobe warns. "You gon' need me one day, w-watch."

"Anyway," Tiff cuts the half-fake, half-real tension growing in the air. "Y'all remember the last one Minah came to? That joint was fuuuun! Remember? That shit felt like a Chief Keef video." We all crack up at this, knowing exactly what she means. From all the mysterious red cups smuggled behind the faraway trees in the picnic area of Oak Community Park next to the rec center. All the "walks" the older kids took near the playground, far away from the grown folks' tables. They'd make sure the dankness rising above their cyphers faded far before anybody noticed the cause for my cousins returning with pink eyes.

"Yeeeah, we was way too lit to be around all those old folks," Maleek adds, a smile creeping back up on his face. "Yo, 'member Mama gettin' pushed in the pool with all her clothes on?" he asks, looking over at Kobe, who starts smiling, too. "That shit was funny as hell till she climbed back out." Kobe's smile leaves just as quick as it came. Maleek still can't disguise how funny it was, even while looking at his brother, who doesn't see what's so funny. "You was laughing *hard* till you peeped that one of Mama's titties popped out. Damn near tackled her with Minah's towel." Maleek says the last part of this laughing so hard it turns into the wheeze of an eighty-year-old smoker who been smoking his whole life. Newports, specifically. Maleek is the biggest chimney I know. Probably why he be so upbeat most of the time. You can't ever really get mad at a dude who seems happy around the clock in the middle of all this chaos. I notice Kobe's hand's tightened around the arm of the couch. It looks right at home on top of all the shredded fabric that Nana's cats have torn through. Kobe don't play about Aunty Jo. Nobody gets to laugh at her. Even when it's lighthearted. Sometimes it seems like he wishes she never was brought up at all, even though he's the one who's always doing it. Maleek clears his throat.

"Everybody was on one," Tiff adds. "Nana called herself tryna make us all stand in one line to wait for the food that took forever to set up. Then had the nerve to get mad when we all started using both sides of the tables to make our plates. We all family, but we a greedy-ass family and none of us was about to wait a whole hour for burgers and pasta salad."

"I don't kn-kn-know what the hell you talkin' 'bout. I would wait for *three* hours just for a s-slice of Aunty Sandy's peach cob—" Kobe starts, quickly stopping himself the minute we lock eyes again. He lowers his voice almost to a whisper. "Yo, my bad, I didn't mean to . . . I—I wasn't tryin' to . . . my bad, Minah. I ain't mean to bring her up like that." Each of us find the spaces in between our fingers way more interesting than talkin' about the person Kobe just brought into the room. Or, more like, the person whose name somebody finally said aloud. Finally.

"So, even when I'm here, y'all gonna act like no one should talk to me about it? It's real, isn't it? Cancer, *right*?" I search all their faces for my answers and no one's bold enough to give me one. Fuckin' cowards. "Nobody had the balls to call me and now I'm right here and all y'all know how to do is joke about everything?! What a surprise," I say, getting up to pace the room. I had imagined myself storming out of whatever room this came up in. On the plane here I told myself, if anybody tries to play games with me, I'm walking out and never coming back. But who was I kidding? I'm stranded here, held hostage by my own family. I lose any chance of getting to the bottom of this mess if I leave without swimming through all the family BS. All the jokes and small talk wrapped tightly around every family secret like a straitjacket. The sourness of room one brings me back into the basement where six pairs of glassy eyes follow me, the air still full of a weighted emptiness. Everybody's smacked. My sneakers feel heavy on the ground. Almost like I'd just walked through a bunch of mud. "Why didn't anybody call me?"

"Everybody thought Nana was the right person to call you first.

Then when she said she tried and couldn't get through, she told Fatimah to do it but she couldn't get through, either," Tiff says, trying to explain for the group. "Don't you remember? You blocked almost everybody after . . . after everything that happened." Tiff is sensitive and already looks like she's holding back a flood. She looks over at Maleek, who has his face in his hands. Then at Kobe, who looks like he can't stand himself for even opening his mouth. Somebody needs to answer me.

"Who called Pop, huh? WHO?!"

TWELVE

Instead of the woman across the hall from me and Pop's
apartment yelling at someone in Trinidad over the phone, I wake
to the sound of clanking pots, running faucets, and a heavy haze of
bacon and eggs coming from below.

Somehow it all rises up to the third floor where Kobe dropped all
my things for me to stay for the next few days. Far above the kitchen
and most of the usable bedrooms, I blink my eyes open realizing
the nightmare wasn't a dream at all: I'm in Sandra's old bedroom,
wrapped in blankets that once absorbed her morning breath after
she moved out of our old house and back here. I'm really here in her
bed. Sun rays force themselves between bent blinds and reflect off
the smeared vanity mirror above the dresser across from the bed. The
sharpness of the light makes it hard for me to go back to sleep. Now
that I remember where I am, the thought of pulling these sheets over
my head makes my skin crawl. A fist slams three times into the door.
"Nana say come get a plate before she feeds it to Smoky!" Nana used
to always threaten to feed our food to a cat when me and Fatimah
were young.

"I'ma be down in a minute," I tell the voice that I can't make out
yet, knowing I ain't goin' down there no time soon. I hear feet plop
all the way down the creaky carpeted stairs that all of us have peed
on at least once. When I'm sure whoever-it-was closed the door at the

bottom of the steps, I open the door and peek out into the hallway, a little afraid of what I might see. When you're small, everything looks like a monster in the dark. Everything was a monster on the third floor when we were kids. Especially in the mysterious extra bedrooms.

Last night Nana told me she'd set clean towels out for me and, by that, she meant there was a mountain of clean laundry on top of the naked mattress in the forgotten bedroom next to Sandra's. The one to the left when you come out into the hallway, across from the Scary-Ass Bathroom on the Third Floor. Back when me and Fatimah were in kindergarten, we'd dare each other to go into this extra bedroom and see who could last the longest without running back out, screaming, sure we'd seen a ghost or some random object move.

This morning, the wooden door creaks when I push it open to the same setup I remember looking up to see from a much smaller body. There's clothing piles everywhere, sorted out in different categories that only Nana understands, but I knew the one on top of the naked bed would still be the clean laundry. No telling what the others are for, but the room smells like the Goodwill. That stale smell that could only come from a mixture of different people's BO clashing together in a sea of things they don't want anymore. I pull a pink towel and a matching washcloth from the top of the laundry pile and almost run-walk back out.

I tiptoe back across the hallway to the bathroom and immediately remember why I never messed with the Scary-Ass Bathroom on the Third Floor if I could help it. Everything about it is the same. From the ugly pink-tiled walls to the matching ugly pink-tiled floors to the matching ugly pink sink to the matching ugly pink tub to the matching ugly pink toilet, this bathroom is on-brand for Nana. But always too cold and everything too big, it's every kid's nightmare. You couldn't tell baby Minah that she wasn't gon' somehow fall backward and drown in the giant toilet with no one around to save her.

With all that I remember it being, my feet are still shocked at the cold of the old tile as I walk across it to sit on the toilet. Even the inside of the toilet is pink. I peer around me, wondering who uses all the space that once was Sandra's. When I'm not here, who is here to hate it just as much? I quickly decide that I'll use the sink to wash up and brush my teeth, the way Nana had taught us to, so I can skip my usual shower. I have to get out of here as soon as possible. Nana says I should be grateful I have the whole third floor to myself, even though it feels like I'm up here with a spirit trying to haunt me.

———

Smoky is cleaning his paws just as I get down to the first floor. I'm lucky there's five different opened boxes of cereal on the kitchen table, but there's way more to move around now that Nana's in cookout mode. I hear her outside ordering everybody to make themselves useful while she preps to fill the van with everything she's accumulated for the re-union. On top of the regular boxes still scattered around the kitchen, there's now boxes of orange T-shirts, paper plates, red plastic cups, burger buns, and chips—and there are several random dodgeballs rolling around. On the counters, silver trays of marinated raw chicken, seasoned raw beef patties, spaghetti, and potato salad are stacked high beside a sink full of still-soaking black-eyed peas. Nana limps into the kitchen, coming in from the back door, even slower than last night. She sort of collapses into the folding chair just inside the kitchen door and lets out a dramatic sigh just before leaning her cane up against the counter. Either Nana is about to lecture me about somethin' or she's gonna take this as another opportunity to size me up even more.

"Well, look who finally decided to join us . . . too bad Smoky was a little too hongry this mornin'." A jab.

"Yeah, guess I had a little jet lag from the flight." A lie.

"Aw, baby, Michigan is Eastern Daylight Time jus' like New York City. Jet lag is when it's a big time difference," she says slyly, flicking her eyes up at me. From where she sits, below me, Nana seems so much smaller than the last time I saw her. Her voice comes out with a little less bass but with just enough edge to know when she's tryna shame somebody. "If you don't wanna be here . . ."

"I'm cool with bein' here, Nana. Just a little tired."

"Well, there's a lot to do so I hope you done gettin' all that rest you don't need. Kobe and Maleek outside loading the van." She pulls an orange T-shirt from one of the boxes near her feet, looks at the tag for a less than a second, and chucks it up at me. She already has hers on, pulled down over her wide hips and an ankle-length denim skirt. There's a dusting of baby powder peeking out from under her collar, but sweat has already started pooling under her armpits and she dabs her forehead with a nearby dish towel. I hold the XS T-shirt out in front of me, then dip into the guest bathroom to pull it over my head while Nana waits in the kitchen to be the mirror I ain't ask for, ready to tell me how I look when I open the door. I look at myself being hugged way too tight but I let Nana see me the way she wants to see me for now. I'll grab a medium before we leave. "I see you fillin' out just like yo' mama. I don't know why you got be hidin' under all them clothes."

I let Nana mumble to herself as she shuffles back into the kitchen. I hear her shoving boxes closer to the back door for me to carry outside. I read the design sprawled across my chest: JOHNSON-WILLIAMS 2019 FAMILY REUNION, and I'm nearly blinded by the way the color combination clashes with this clip-art-ass design. The only thing that's gon' save this look is a pair of overalls. I turn to get a look at the other side of the shirt and realize a collage of heads are screen-printed on the back. It only takes about thirty seconds for me to understand what they all have in common: they're dead, with Sandra's head the largest at the center. Something like an ice-cold punch hits my shoulder and soaks the whole left side of my body before I can see what's going on.

I chase Kobe all the way down the hallway until he leads me out to the front porch where Maleek and a bunch of kids I don't know stand surrounding me with water balloons, Super Soakers, and buckets. An ambush. I turn back around, nearly knocking Nana's candy cart over trying to get to the stairs with no time to look behind me. I slam the door at the bottom of the stairs from the inside just in time.

"You know Nana ain't havin' no locked doors in her house!" the kid who's chasing me back in here says.

"Y'all wrong for this!"

All of us pour out the back of Nana's funky van like the breath of a Baptist church usher leaned in too close, asking you spit your gum out into their glove. The heat beats down on every part my skin, but my hair saves me a little, unlike Kobe. Though the pamphlets Nana sits out on one of the picnic tables says the reunion starts at eleven, Kobe is drenched and already complaining at nine thirty when we start setting up the extra chairs, tables, and food under the shaded pavilion. That's where most of the elders will post up all day, gossiping about Reverend Ernie and the choir director he be makin' eyes at.

Nana puts me in charge of blowing up most of the orange and purple balloons 'cause she says I still got "pure lungs," unlike my "raggedy cousins" who don't do nothin' but defile their bodies and eat up all her food. She says the Lord can still use me. But I'm folded over my knees at one of the tables, winded, after blowing up only five. I push myself to make it to ten and give up as cars start pulling up along the street, each vehicle spilling out kids and grown folks, most of whom are completely unrecognizable to me. Must be second, third, and fourth cousins on Sandra's side, once-removed.

"You are kidding meee. You are kidding me, Delores! That is NOT baby Minah over there lookin' all grown," I hear Aunty Jo say behind me. I smell her before I even realize what's going on. She scoops me into a hug I ain't ask for before I'm even fully turned around to see her. Whichever Avon perfume she got on today mushes into my chest as she screams through our entire hug. When I'm finally able to free myself of her death grip, she don't let me go that far. Instead, she holds me out in front of her like something she's thinkin' about buying at a store that's way too expensive for her. "Sheeeit, and you taller than me now? I don't care how grown you is," she says, still looking me up and down, "I used to be the one that cleaned that behind when ya mama couldn't and you always gon' be my baby." In comes another hug, her scent frying the inside of my nose.

"Hey, Aunty," I squeeze out.

"'Hey?' That must be that New York City lingo. Minah don' gone off and got New York on us now," she says as if somehow the way I say anything is different from everybody else just because I don't live here anymore. Both her hands slide down my arms so she can grab my hands and step even closer into my space. "You doin' all right, baby?" she whispers. "I know you getting' big and all and you got a whole new life now but you know you can always call your Aunty Jo, right? I'm always here for you, baby. Whatever you need."

"I'm okay, Aunty."

"You sure?" She stares up at me searching my eyes for weakness. Maybe she hopes I'll crack and cry right there. Aunty Jo dresses just like Nana, but instead of ankle-length denim skirts, she's got her reunion T-shirt tucked into some high-waist mom jeans two sizes too big for her, held up by an overly tightened belt to give the illusion of a Coke bottle figure. She pushes her thick glasses further up on her nose and pulls a napkin out of her pocket to dab the sweat building up across her forehead. The sound of more car doors slamming saves me from having to answer, just seconds before I might have said what I really think about her question and that it's five years too late. Aunty Jo stops waiting for an answer and pats my shoulder before patting her bra down for what I already knew would be money. She grabs one of my hands and I open it to a sweaty, folded five-dollar bill as she makes her way back to Nana.

Johnson-Williams family reunions pretty much been the same as far back as I remember. For the first two hours or so, mad cars pull up and park alongside the tree-lined streets surrounding the park. Aunties, uncles, cousins, and grandparents scatter in all directions while the oldest kids get forced to help carry anything heavy to the pavilion, where Nana's put plastic coverings on all the tables and set up extra chairs. Because a lot of the food gets cooked all the way up until the last minute—remember: there were uncooked black-eyed peas still soaking in the sink—these early hours are just all of us waiting for Nana to let us eat while we make small talk with blood relatives that we're supposed to know, but don't. Which is why most of us who've graduated from the kiddie tables to being able to do whatever the hell we want are tryna find somewhere to dip. Before all the awkward introductions, followed by every elder in our family taking their turn at describing how much we've grown beyond the babies they wish we still were.

Nana grabs my hand and leads me over to where she's setting up the Sterno heaters all the way down the middle of an extra-long picnic table situated at the front of the pavilion. In about an hour, both sides will be lined with all kinds of hands reaching for barbecue ribs, fruit salad, Hawaiian rolls, and baked beans piled just high enough to feed close to one hundred of us. Kobe and Maleek are putting long tin trays in wire racks above each Sterno, then filling them with water, while Nana starts showcasing me to everybody who once knew me as a baby.

"This your great-uncle Bernie. 'Member Uncle Bernie?"

"Hi, Uncle Bernie," I say, peering at a man who looks a lot like Nana in the face.

"Oh, wow. You sho' is Sandra's baby, from the cheeks to the eyes. Got her legs, too," he says with a quick wink. He adjusts his pants and licks his lips as Nana pushes past him and pulls me behind her to the next person. The park is starting to get so full that music blasts from a whole bunch of directions at the same time like the speakers are battling it out for our attention. Fred Hammond, a voice I've known prolly since I was in Sandra's belly, blasts from Nana's CD player at the edge of the drink table while Kobe's turned on 105.1 to blast it from Nana's van, something he'd never get away with if she didn't have all these people distracting her.

From a distance, I catch small clouds of smoke escaping a white Dodge Challenger parked behind a giant maple tree next to the playground. The speakers are turned up so high the bass sounds like it's rattling the car and everybody who's in it. Tiff pulls up and parks right in front of the Dodge before stepping out and bouncing her ass randomly to the sound of it as she walks toward us like she's at the club.

And she definitely looks like she's headed to the club after this, arriving in cutoff shorts that look like denim panties and a reunion T-shirt she's turned into a crop top, shredded and dangling beads over her partly exposed belly. One false move and her whole coochie could fall out. I hear Nana suck her teeth, and her disapproval sounds like she wishes the Lord would let her call her play niece something ungodly. Tiff's gripping at least five chip-filled grocery bags in each hand and Nana's already nagging about how these useless men around here ain't helping her bring them from the car.

"It's cool, Granny. I'm strong. I don't need these ni—boys," she says, catching herself. It's then that I notice the girl Tiff said she'd be bringing, lagging behind in her shadow. She looks just like Young Ma, the way Tiff had first described her, then shown me in the pictures on her phone before she left Nana's last night. Baby is what Tiff had called her. From behind her, Baby looks me up and down, grazing the three long whiskers on her chin, using her other hand to grab her crotch. Her shoulders are hiked up close to her ears like she's tryna perform confidence even though it makes her look as insecure and awkward as a teenage boy going through puberty, unsure of what to do with his own body. I catch a flash of gold sparkling from Baby's bottom row of teeth when she notices Nana's glare burning a hole into her face the way she does any young person who acts like they can't speak in her presence. Especially one who she thinks looks like a dude but ain't steppin' up the way she thinks one should. Nana glances down at Baby's empty hands for a brief moment and lets out a loud sigh that sounds like she don't even wanna know who this random person Tiff dragged in here is.

"Keep tellin' yourself that, baby. One day you gon' be jus' as tired as I am, jus' wantin' someplace to sit yo ass down somewhere," Nana says before pointing Tiff to where the chip bowls are. "One day you gon' be tired of runnin' around here with these gold-chain-wearin' smiley-ass good-for-nothins and you gon' want somebody strong enough to let you rest." Baby slips her gold chain under her white tee and grazes her cornrows with her hand. "But you right, though. You still young and useful. Come tie this apron at the back for your nana," she says. "What you over here all up under me for, Minah? You been gone too damn long to be actin' like a stranger now that you're here," she says, nudging me away from her as if she hadn't been exploiting me for cheap labor just seconds ago. Nana wants me to be useful but then wants me not to be too busy to mingle with family members I probably only saw once when I was a bay but am supposed to remember. She wants to use all my youthful strength but wants to parade me around as her grandbaby who's all grown up now, living in a big city. I decide to take a long lap around the park by myself while Tiff and Baby pick up where I left off with the balloons. Unlike me, she only smokes weed socially and could handle the job much better. I don't need Nana getting suspicious about what I'm doing with my lungs.

Walking out from under the pavilion, I step directly into the blazing sunshine, the sun now much higher than it was when we first pulled up. I feel like I'm walking down a *Soul Train* line of all the family reunion elements, one by one. First, the charcoal smoke coming off the grill that Uncle James is firing up. The first hint of barbecue fills the air with a batch of heavily seasoned chicken legs and burger patties. I rush past him, pulling my twists out of my hair tie and letting them fall around my face so he doesn't recognize me just yet. Next, cigarette smoke being carried by the wind from the other side of the street where family that regularly gets shamed for their tobacco addiction get their fix before walking over. I pat my jeans to feel for the box I'd tucked into my pocket before we left Nana's. Then there's the bubbles flying up and floating everywhere coming from the kids sitting at the playground's edge, blowing into neon-colored circles, trying to see who could blow the biggest ones before they pop. Me and Fatimah used to come in the house with splinters and scrapes from all the wood-chip shavings that covered the ground just under the swings that dangle behind them.

Past the playground, people start throwing down blankets, lawn chairs, and personal coolers right under the trees with the most shade as kids zigzag between picnic tables covered in art supplies, candy, jugs of red drink, and tipped-over plastic cups. A little bit further out, closer to the forest area, a few older kids set up buckets of water balloons, a rainbow-colored blow-up kiddie pool, and a long green water slide with a sprinkler connected to the hose they'd pulled from the other side of the bathrooms at the far corner of the park. Toddlers already dressed in their bathing suits sit cross-legged, sucking on Popsicles with their eyes glazed over waiting to be told they can play. I guess this'll make up for there being no real pool this time.

Sandra wore her nursing uniform to the last Johnson-Williams family reunion I went to six years ago. But there'd been a rumor going around that she'd been fired from the hospital weeks before. Depending on who she was talking to, she either still worked there or she was interviewing at other places and wanted to dress for the job that was hers. I remember her going off about how—even though she wasn't wearing the family T-shirt—she should be recognized for her commitment to that year's colors: light blue and dark blue. Every nurse in Obsidian wore light blue scrubs. Sandra's personality was so big and full of laughter that I always wanted to believe whatever she was saying, even after all the drama with her and Pop, and it seemed like telling stories about jobs and friends she ain't have no more made her feel good. Plus, I was ten. What did I know about how jobs and people worked? She was my mama, so how could anything she said have been a lie?

We'd taken over the entire Obsidian Community & Culture Center that year. I remembered great-aunties sneaking judgmental looks out the corner of their eyes in the locker room at my older cousins who'd just grown booties and titties the winter before. While they pushed their press and curls into hideous flowered swimming caps and squeezed themselves into skirted swimsuits, my already-sexed-up teenage cousins strutted past them in skimpy polka-dot string bikinis, capless and carefree, out to the pool area where my uncles complained about them walkin' around here actin' too damn grown. I knew they were already having sex, overhearing grown folks say that's what you could credit for their freshly widened hips and curves. I remember seeing the way Uncle James eyeballed the older girls' bare bellies, his distraction with their bodies almost making me forget he was their mama's brother and had at least twenty years on them. Kobe and Maleek weren't as obvious but they found ways to play-fight with my older girl cousins, giving them an excuse to grab and throw them into the pool. I'd watch them pop back up from under the water loudly complaining that they'd messed up their hair, making a whole show of it like they were mad but secretly loving all the extra attention. They'd gotten their hair braided into protective styles the week before specifically so getting dropped into the pool wouldn't be a problem. Those dramatics weren't foolin' nobody.

Sandra had let all of us know she wasn't about to get in nobody's pool. She'd found her a spot on a plastic beach chair next to it, though. She'd kicked off her white Crocs and fell asleep with one hand wrapped around a red cup, the other nursing a lit Marlboro Light. The rec-center staff warned there was to be no eating, drinking, or smoking in the pool area, but Sandra always did whatever the hell she wanted. I was relieved to see she'd already dozed off when I came out the locker room, hiding myself under the large neon-yellow beach towel that swallowed me up in all its color. Under it, no one could see my rapidly changing body, no one had a real reason to stare. I'd thought I'd be so cute in my black-and-white-striped bathing suit when I tried it on at home, but next to all my teenage cousins, I felt as round and boyish as a referee. I wasn't gon' take that towel off until I was only steps outside the water. I tried to tiptoe past Sandra, but noting the lit cigarette, I stopped to pull it from her fingers so I could put it out to avoid yet another burn hole in her work clothes. And as if she could feel her favorite thing being snatched from her in her dreams, her eyes opened just in time to ask me to get her another beer.

THIRTEEN

"Here," Tiff says, handing me a red cup.

I don't even have to look down to know what it is. Or why she's probably gonna tell me to "be cool and come on." I take a sip and try to do what she says as the whiskey burns the whole way down my throat. Tiff and Baby don't wait for me after this command. They just walk back across the park, through the pavilion, to a picnic table on the other side where Kobe, Maleek, and our cousin Jacob are at what looks like the tail end of a heated game of UNO, judging by how few cards Jacob has in his hands and the look on Kobe's face. Maleek hovers over his hand full of cards while it's hard to tell what Kobe has. We sit around the players, each of us choosing one shoulder to look over as Jacob throws out a yellow five and a blue five, the blue card on top.

"Shouldna did dat," Kobe smirks, throwing down three blue draw twos.

"Fuck!" Maleek must have thought he was close to catching up to Jacob. He draws his cards, organizing what he now has in his hands, and looks over at Jacob, who looks like he might have caught some bad luck, too. Until he throws down blue skip, a red skip, and a red one.

"UNO out," Jacob says, stepping away from the table and taking a lap around it clapping for himself. Kobe takes a sip out of his cup and doesn't say anything. We only have ever seen Jacob at family reunions. He lives with Aunty Sharon in Memphis, Tennessee, where they moved when we were all just babies. Taller than all the other boys in the family, we know he got most of his height from his daddy, who left when he was five to play pro ball overseas and just never came back. Winning was way more important to Jacob than to Kobe or Maleek, even though being beat by him got on Kobe's nerves every time. Kobe was always convinced each game he won was rigged.

"H-h-how we know you ain't cheat, m-m-muhfucka?" He asks. "Your shuffling skills always been a lil off. How the hell you end up w-w-with all them special cards?"

"What we really should be askin' is why you such a sore loser, cuz."

"Yeah," Maleek chimes in, backing Kobe up for once. "How the fuck you got all them good cards? Don't nobody hand be that good through a whole game." Kobe never looks like he's joking, while Maleek just looks like he's talking shit, the way you're supposed to while you're playing cards. I know Tiff didn't walk me all the way over to play, too. I've only become good at the talking-shit part. And I don't even feel like doing that. Jacob moves on like he doesn't have time for people who can't accept that it's their destiny to lose.

"How long she gon' be here?" he asks Maleek, as if he couldn't just ask me directly.

"Prolly 'bout as long as you," I answer for myself. Jacob puts his hands up in surrender. All around us smoke from the grill starts to accumulate and my stomach starts screamin'. Luckily, we see Aunty Sharon walking around the park, already barefooted, rounding everybody up for the prayer I'd wished we would skip, but this family likes a side of church with all our dysfunction. We can't all fit under the pavilion awning but we try, as Nana informs us all that Uncle James will lead us in saying grace over the food.

I study Uncle James with his arm wrapped around Nana as she

leans into the crease of his armpit. She's already dabbing at her eyes.
The smallest kids make their way to the center, in front of them, and
sit on the ground while everybody else crowds around. The pavilion
smells like too many different colognes, perfumes, deodorants, pow-
ders, all on top of grilled meats and burning nag champa incense
stuck to the posts and in the soil at all four corners. Jacob throws an
arm around my shoulder and leans in to tell me he's glad to see me all
grown up now.

I pick up one of the reunion pamphlets from the floor and look
through it to see what the rest of this day is supposed to be like, forgetting that it might remind me why I came here in the first place. Sandra
is on the cover, clip-art bouquets framing her face and the years 1982–
2019 below her name with some bible verse I can't remember under
that. She looks just like she did when she was alive. Or at least as close
as you can get with faded printer ink. I open the pamphlet to a collage of pictures from past family reunions, a bunch of us smiling and
laughing the way people expect families to feel together. The program
says Nana has some important announcement to make after we all eat,
toward the end, but that don't make any sense. We gon' be eating till
we leave here. Ain't no bottom to our stomachs with all this food covering every table in front of us, waiting to be pigged out on in between
conversations about nothing and everything at the same time. It's the
food we all here for. And even after we've eaten so much we have to
unbutton our pants and doze off under the trees in between, Nana's
gonna send a bunch of us home with to-go sweet potato pies she made
and plastic containers full of potato salad and ribs.

Uncle James asks us to bow our heads and everybody goes quiet. In
the pamphlet, this is when it says Deacon Durrell will lead us in a moment of silence in honor of Sandra. Deacon Durrell is Uncle James's

daddy and I've only ever seen him in moments of silence. He's one of those deacons who never speaks but always got a permanent chair onstage at church just above the altar. He looks like he could end up as the face of one of these pamphlets any day now with those Coke-bottle glasses and gray sideburns preserved from the seventies. A few hats come off my cousins' heads and adults pull kids who can't calm down on their own close to their bodies. I focus my eyes down on the ground where everybody dead goes and start wondering what part of that was up to god. Uncle James says a bunch of words we were taught in our family's church that might as well be in another language the way it makes my brain go off somewhere else. And then he starts to call out all the names of our new ancestors. Markus Johnson, Alisha Williams, Sandra Okar . . . My fist clenches as he names her as if the divorce never happened. As if she'd never switched up on us. On me. After the list, Deacon Durrell says, "A moment," and then there's nothing but the soft jingle of the wind chimes dangling from the wooden roof above us and the squeak of empty swings blowing in the wind.

I stopped closing my eyes during prayer and moments of silence years ago when I realized the Lord wasn't coming to save me from whatever had gotten ahold of Sandra. And if the Lord is even real, closing my eyes ain't something I should have to do around Him. Whatever the Lord is gon' do, He can do in front me and if He can't, then I need to keep watch. When everybody else closes their eyes in prayer, to respect the Lord or whatever, I look around all the bowed heads. Nana is dabbing even harder at all the water now pouring from her face. As her shoulders start to bounce and the crying gets loud enough for all of us to hear, people around her start to pat her back and mumble things into her ears. I expected this kind of drama but I didn't think I'd feel so lonely in it. Nobody reaches for my back. No one even touches or looks Fatimah's way. Maybe people think it's worse to lose somebody you birthed than to lose the person who birthed you. When I look over at Fatimah, she seems annoyed with Robyn, bouncing her on one hip before switching to the other. She keeps shuffling her body around, trying to make sure her baby doesn't interrupt the moment with her cries until she bows out of the moment of silence altogether. I wish I had a good excuse.

Sweaty bodies start moving around me, snapping me out of the trance I put myself in to endure the sadness show. Kids slam themselves into tall adult legs, forcing their way to the front of the line that's growing at one end of the long food table and the only reason I sort of rush toward it is so I have something to do before another relative I don't know appears in front of me. I scan the table for the shit I can eat, which might be only a fourth of the table. Smoked barbecue ribs, grilled hamburger patties, spicy Polish sausages, and charred Koegel's Viennas hot dogs take up half the table before we get to everything else: Nana's famous potato salad, sweet coleslaw, pasta salad, roasted corn on the cob, five-cheese baked mac and cheese, and a marshmallowy fruit salad at the end. The table closes out with a spread of buns, Hawaiian rolls, chips, plasticware, and five coolers full of pop, beer, iced tea, and undoubtedly a few bottles of liquor somebody tucked under all the ice where Nana can't find them.

I stack my plate with pasta salad and corn after telling the fifth auntie that I'm sure I don't want anything else and that "no, I'm not gonna still be hungry," even though I know that's a lie. My stomach growls thinking about Kobe refusing to take me to the store last night for veggie patties when I realized ain't nobody thinking about no vegan shit at a cookout. Nana eyeballs my plate on my way out from under the pavilion and makes some comment about it being the reason why I don't have no ass or titties. At the other end of the park, I find a spot under a tree closest to the playground with the wood chips so I can eat my corn on the cob in peace. A girl swings her body across the monkey bars far above the ground where a bunch of other kids are playing tag. Robyn comes running toward the group of kids and almost gets caught up in all the running legs just before Fatimah comes running behind her to sweep her up.

"I can watch her for you . . . you know, if you wanna go eat or something," I offer.

"First thing Mama taught us when we was young is not to go off with strangers," she says through her teeth, her voice lowered almost like she's talking to Robyn. Maybe she is. She could have been talking to anybody the way she says it without looking at me.

"I'm not a—" But she keeps walking and finds a spot on a bench on the other side of the playground, where she whispers something to Robyn just before letting her crawl her way into the sandbox with a few other toddlers covered in dirty city sand. I wonder if that sandbox still got all the red ants in it. Red ants bite. We learned that back in the third grade when Sandra let us play hopscotch outside Nana's house barefoot. Fatimah paused on the number four and screamed, thinking a sharp rock had dug up in her heel, but Nana knew different. Came running out the front door when she heard Fatimah crying and cussed Sandra out in her absence for letting us "run around like some type of country-ass little kids who don't know nothin' about the city." Nana always had something to say about the way Sandra was raising us when she wasn't around.

Fatimah leans back against the park bench at the same time I rest against the tree bark and pulls her phone out to scroll the way all of us do whenever we need to tune out the world. Right now, that world is me. And maybe her kid, but Robyn seems like too much of a hassle. I can't believe my sister has a kid.

I pull out my phone to back-to-back texts from Nikki. I close my eyes for a second before I disappear into her world. It almost feels like the competing sounds of the park enter me from all sides just like the breeze does my hair, now pulled up on the top of my head. Migos's "MotorSport" vibrates out the all-black car that both Kobe and Maleek now sit on top of. Maleek hops off the hood, walks over to Fatimah, and hands her whatever's left in his red cup, shuffling back to the car to the beat of the song. Nicki Minaj's voice blares over the speakers, telling us to watch our mouths, and Fatimah mouths the lyrics in my direction, jutting her neck forward to the rhythm, and then switches her attention back to her phone. Mary Mary's "Walking" echoes off surrounding tree trunks from the other side of the field where they've set up subwoofers closer to the Slip 'N Slide. Far enough for the younger kids to not be contaminated by whatever demons had already gotten into the rest of us. As if the songs are bouncing off each other, the gospel lyrics ask us if we're getting it wrong or right. Another van pulls up blasting the Isley Brothers, drowning both songs out, and an elder too old to know he's too old tries to start a *Soul Train* line near the grill. He's telling every child in sight that they don't know nothin' about how he used to do it "back in the day."

"Good to see you've missed us," Aunty Jo says, hovering over me and my unlocked phone. Her voice is heavy with sarcasm just like her face, scrunched as if she smells something that died under this tree and is debating whether or not she's gon' scoop it up and put it in the garbage. Before I blocked her and everybody else online, she never missed an opportunity to make me feel like trash for not visiting or calling enough. Shame is Aunty Jo's favorite weapon. I don't deny anything she says 'cause her comments ain't far from how I feel. Who gets excited to see somebody who makes you feel bad for growing up and changing? I'm not sorry for not wanting to hang out with boring Aunty Jo. Aunty Jo who tucks in all her T-shirts and whose idea of a good time is overnight lock-in prayer service at any church that will have her. Aunty Jo who hasn't been on a date since the nineties when her and Uncle James split up. And everybody knows Uncle James wasn't never that adventurous so she prolly ain't been on a date ever. She once walked into Nana's TV room where me and Fatimah were watching *Sister, Sister* and turned off an episode where they were getting ready for a double date, telling us that there ain't no reason god-fearing girls should be so pressed about going out on dates with lil boys who only want one thing. By the time we reached middle school we were convinced that Aunty Jo was just gay and would rather tell everybody she's married to the Lord instead of admitting the truth to herself. I look up, squinting my eyes to see her with the sun beaming through the tree branches overhead. There's nothing I can really say to her comment. "You gon' sit under this tree the whole day?"

"I've only been over here for a little bit, Aunty. I wanted to eat in the shade."

"Eat what? Your lil twigs and bread?" she says, gesturing toward my meatless plate.

"I had chips, too," I say, hoping that'll get her off my back.

"I know you got these so-called cultured white folks all over social media telling you that you don't need meat on your plate and that it's bad for the environment and all that, but you know what's really killing us?" Here it comes. "Satan. Ain't nothin' gonna heal us like the blood of Jesus, ya heard?" I let Aunty Jo rock for a while. Honestly, I could sit here in silence for at least ten minutes, and she wouldn't even notice that I'm not responding. I don't think I have the energy to make it that long this time, though.

"You made the coleslaw? It was so good I think I'ma get some more in minute. And not a *single* raisin in it like how these white folks be out here makin' it," I add, so she feels like we're on the same page a little. She blushes, brushing imaginary crumbs or dust off the waist of her jeans, proud.

"Yeah, I did a lil sum'n," she says, falling for my bait. Over her shoulder, I start to see everybody walking back toward the pavilion just seconds after all the music gets turned off. My body feels relieved that this means I no longer have to sit under Aunty Jo's judgmental gaze even though it also means we'll be gathered too close again to wait for whatever Nana's big announcement is. Out the corner of my eye I see Fatimah throw back the last gulp from Maleek's cup and tell Robyn to come on. She doesn't wait and starts walking across the field with her eyes still glued to her phone while Robyn rushes to climb back out of the sandbox behind her. I take my time standing up to make my way back over but not too much. I've got to blend in with everybody enough for Nana not to be able to spot me in the crowd if she happens to try to throw my name in whatever she has to say.

As I get closer, a small hand grabs the side of my overalls and tugs. I look down and, seeing that it's Robyn, look around before slowing down to see what she wants. She smiles and grabs my hand, flipping it over. With the other hand she drops a fistful of smooshed dandelions and sand into my hand, then runs. Looking back up toward the pavilion, I catch Fatimah glaring at me as she yanks Robyn up off the ground. As I get closer, I see everybody shifting away from the center at the same time that an almost-unbearable stench of pee and liquor fills our nostrils. Nana, who was walking in the same direction that the smell seems to be coming from, stops in her tracks while Uncle James walks in between her and the smell. I finally get close enough to recognize the old man who's brought this smell here, seeing his face full of long gray hair with a very familiar paper cup still in his hand, an old baseball cap pulled off and in the other. He lifts the hand with the baseball cap to scratch at the collar of an orange T-shirt that looks like he found it in a dumpster, then grabs at his sagging purple sweatpants. The pants are at least two sizes too big. And, strangely, too new. Nana looks frozen in space.

"Benny?"

FOURTEEN

"It's so good seeing all y'all's beautiful faces today," Nana says between big breaths that seem to be exhausting her.

Kobe's put a hand out for Nana to hold while he guides her to stand on top of what was a kiddie table just an hour ago. She's up there leaning on her cane, looking everywhere but at us, like she's waiting for everybody to calm down the way a teacher does for a class that won't shut up. Uncle James has the old man—Benny, I guess—pulled to the side, far enough away so that we can no longer smell him, and is piling as much food as he can onto three different plates. He'll probably stack them the way Nana does just before wrapping to-go plates with foil. I want to dap him up for somehow finding a way to whisper whatever he's saying to the old man and braving the possibility of catching whatever homeless people pick up living on the streets. I can't take my eyes off him or stop wondering how he made it all the way here from the grocery store parking lot. It always seems like homeless people live wherever I've seen them beg the most. I've only seen him once and it wasn't around here. Maybe he caught wind this was happening today somehow and made a whole-ass Obsidian pilgrimage for food people are less likely to keep from him. Everybody's supposed to be in a good, giving mood at these, so he prolly figured nobody would turn him away. No way to hide how much extra we got. Of everything. "Some of y'all I ain't seen in . . . ages," Nana continues, staring directly at me.

Now's the first time I notice Nana's everything is matching just how she always has. Just didn't have time to look at her before we left. Her cane is completely covered in orange and purple tape, striped like a misfit candy cane. Her socks, burnt orange. One shoe, burnt-orange laces. The other shoe, purple laces. Her lipstick, a sparkly purple that looks like she borrowed it from one of the kids running around her house that I don't know. Her arm, covered in what looks like all the bangles she could find at the annual African Art Festival that they usually have in that same parking lot where the old man tapped on Tiffany's window when I was asleep. I glance over where he and Uncle James were standing a few minutes ago and he's sucked the meat clean off the third rib from his first plate. He don't look like he's goin' anywhere no time soon. He mumbles something to himself, laughs, and wipes the barbecue grease off his lips with the back of his hand and moves on to a lemon-pepper chicken wing while Uncle James stands watch about ten feet away with his arms crossed over his chest. He looks like an underpaid security guard waiting for something exciting to happen.

"Sandra would be so happy to see this. All of us together again like we used to do. She'd be so happy to see us all together, eatin', smilin', runnin' around here with all these youngins. Probably would have been makin' her rounds at all the tables tryna make y'all your second and third plates," Nana says before being taken over by a short coughing fit. Kobe pulls out her inhaler and she coughs one more time, then spits behind the table, before taking two pulls from the pump. "It's been such a loooong time since this park done looked like this," she says. It sounds like Nana is taking shots at me every other sentence, as if I'm the only one who's skipped more than one of these things. You'd think I'm the reason our family has so much trouble staying together like a dried-up cookie. Even with most of us squeezed up under here right now, everybody is separated into groups with the people they came with. Each group having they own little party, only brushed up against one another's arms in random moments for the free food, everything made a little bit less tense by the secret bottles, cups, and blunts passed person to person like unwanted children you play with, then leave with somebody else.

"I'm so glad so many of us could make it this time so I could share some family business with y'all. It's time for me to sell the house. I'm letting it go. And before y'all start—"

It's too late. A collection of *hell noes!* and *the fucks?!* and *Granny can't do this!* spread throughout the crowd, and it feels like the park turns into a rowdy cafeteria full of black kids their white teachers can't quiet or handle. Nana stands still, hovering above us but shrinking under our collective disapproval. Well, theirs. Not mine. Sandra's dead and now Nana wants to sell the house she grew up in. Go figure. I don't care. She can do whatever the hell she wants to do, just like Sandra did when she got tired of being my mama. Nana slams her cane down on the picnic table three times. "Now, y'all ain't gon' stand in front of me being this disrespectful, is you? I changed many of y'all's stankin'-ass diapers without so much as a thank-you for raising y'all ungrateful behinds."

Everybody gets quiet again but a lot of arms cross over their chests like Uncle James's. Some turn around and start heading back to their cars. Kobe is strangely calm about everything and that makes me nervous. Kobe's the type to explode when you least expect it even though he always says he cool. "Halfa y'all ain't even been over the house to come check in on your granny in years and you mad? Y'all might not want to acknowledge it but yo' granny gettin' old and I'm sick of talkin' to these white folks about my damn house. They offerin' me some real money and I'm in there strugglin' every day to keep this family together and y'all don't do nothin' but find ways to split us up. I'm tired," she says, shifting her weight onto the other foot. "I'm tired of raising y'all by myself. And maybe if I lived somewhere that was just for me, you wouldn't be leaving me to raise y'all's kids, too."

I'm tired of listening to this sad song, so I turn to look behind me. Back at Uncle James on duty watching the old man who Nana called Benny inhale too much food. But when I look, Benny, who I thought would be uncovering foil from his second plate, is walking away, too.

FIFTEEN

My stomach heaves at the smell of eggs taking over Tiffa-ny's apartment. Fried, sunny-side up, "just like they be serving them at brunch downtown," she says.

It wakes me out of some dream I've already forgotten by the time I sit up, shoving the weighted blanket she covered me with laid out on her couch the night before. Something about decaying skulls and Nana's house being taken away, whole, by a pickup truck. I'd swear it was veganism that makes me hate the smell so much, but she tells me I got too twisted last night and that's what hangovers do to light-weights: everything smells like straight-up doo-doo. She says that even if it was pancakes she had on the griddle, I'd still be ready to vomit 'cause my body's mad at my choices. Tiffany don't drink like the rest of us. Says she's seen enough of this family gone off some type of spirit when we should be talking to one another instead, even though she was the last person to push a cup into my hands. But don't nobody in this family talk. Why talk when we can fight and get it over with? LET'S JUST FIGHT: the perfect caption for a Johnson-Williams family meme. But not even Tiffany talks really. At least not about nothin' that serious. Just laughs like our drama is nothing but a joke.

Natural light shines from every wall of Tiff's downtown apart-ment like a Catholic church covered in stained glass, but here everything glows white. The couch. The floor. The ceiling. This bougie-ass weighted blanket that she says calms people who got anxiety real bad. Even the shit she says sometimes sounds white these days. I don't know how a blanket could do anything for me and our family's problems. I don't know how lying under something that's wild heavy could ever suck the heaviness buried deep inside of me. All it seems like it does is make it hard to escape. Which, to me, is the best solution for blood-related problems. What does Tiffany even know? All that white logic and she still eats eggs. Please.

"Girl, it's nine o'clock. You finna sleep all day?"

"Maybe," I reply, serious.

"You been gone so long that you think you could just do whatever you want on a Sunday morning. You know Nana ain't goin' for that. Church is in an hour and if yo' ass ain't in the front pew with the rest of us—"

"What? She gon' whoop me or something? Too old for that. And you heard what she said yesterday. She's tired of keeping this family together. Only reason half of y'all still go with her is to keep this family together. And look: It doesn't even work. I'm going back to sleep." I lay back down, using every drop of hungover energy I have to pull the twenty-pound blanket back over me and face the inside of the couch to scroll my phone. The number of texts from Nikki and Mike has tripled since yesterday. Every time I try to respond it's like I lose any words that they'd understand. Or any words that don't make me sound too depressing. I text Nikki back first. Mike is patient.

Me

oh I see you miss me for real. a bitch gone for

two days and you fallin' apart! lol

Nikki

oh, she's alive. *eye roll*

                                                                              Me
                              don't be like that, fren! you know my fam crazy. ily, girl!

Nikki

yeah yeah yeah. what's good? what's goin' on, sis?

I skip a lot of the extra stuff to get to the parts I think Nikki wants
to hear most: the fact that Fatimah's a mother and her baby, Robyn,
gave me flowers when her mama wasn't looking. The fact that I smoked
some mid in Nana's basement with my cousins. The fact that they had
me sleeping in the literal juices of a very dead Sandra and that the
third-floor bathroom is the perfect place for her spirit to haunt me.
The fact that when I look around it don't seem like much has changed
and that I'm ready to go.

Nikki

Son, my mama told you to pack the smudge stick. Or as least some palo
santo. Sounds like she was right. The third floor sounds demonic, girl.
Rotflmao
But, nah. For real. You okay?

————

It won't come out. No matter how long I sit here. No matter how much
I push. No matter how much water I drink, even though I don't really
remember the last time I did that. All I remember is more red cups
and all us cousins taking walk after walk to the faraway spot in the

park past the largest maple tree while the grown folks argued under the pavilion about who should've got Nana's house. Funny enough, it was Nana's strange remedies that always fixed my constant constipation as a kid and here I am on the toilet; ain't been able to shit since I got here. I'm convinced, now, that it's something in Obsidian's water. One of the many things that's messed up about this dead-end place. I told Nikki and she suggested some tea her mama uses all the time but finding that in the OB sounds like too much work. Especially since it sounds like some earthy-crunchy juju stuff that Nana and all the other church mothers would rebuke. Tiffany bangs on the door for the second time and I flush to pretend I'm finished, then leave the faucet running after washing my hands to drown out the sound of me opening her cabinets.

Tiffany has clear plastic boxes for everything she puts on her face. I don't understand how all this shit is necessary for one person but I'm the last one who'd know. It's been Noxzema and cocoa butter for me since I can remember. Sandra always greased up me and Fatimah, head to toe, after every bath. Had us looking like porcelain dolls each night before bedtime. Soon as we were old enough to take care of our own bodies, Fatimah started asking to pick out her own stuff while I stayed happy with our basic routine, good with not having to roam aisle after aisle tryna figure out which creams or soaps were for black girls who like the color of their skin as it is. I move a few things around to find the box of lipsticks, the only thing I ever saw on Sandra. Push more boxes around looking for medications but find none, amazed at how different Tiffany's cabinet is from how Sandra's was. Every few months there was a new thing she said her doctors had her taking for pain. What pain? It didn't really make a difference. After the headaches and the cramps, it seems like all of us lost track.

I turn off the faucet and open the door just as Tiff's about to bang on it again. She's fully dressed and cussing me out about having to wash her hot spots in the kitchen sink 'cause I took too long. She pushes past me into the bathroom and sits on the toilet seat to lotion her legs while I wander her apartment studying the high ceiling, exposed brick walls, polished cement floor, and plush accent pillows on her bed like I'm a kid in an art museum for the first time. Don't nobody I know live in anything like this in Obsidian. Nobody but Tiff. She yells to me from inside her bedroom, saying something about having to hurry up 'cause we still gotta stop at Nana's house so I can change out the clothes I sinned in last night. I wish I could just skip this part, stay here, and sleep.

———

Life Row Third Pentecostal Christ the King Church smells exactly like it did the last time I was here: stale breath, White Diamond perfume, and old carpet. I'm surprised it's still standing given how small it is. Coming up the road where this church is the only stop, it sits on a hill with its own parking lot and looks like an abandoned house. I'm positive the walls shake as the choir sings the opening praise-and-worship song, being that it makes up over half of the congregation. Only about ten of us sit in the pews being blasted by their morning screams. I'm amazed that they still let Nana take up a whole seat on the praise-and-worship team given that she be needing to use her asthma pump in between every verse. I remember Pastor laying hands on her when me and Fatimah were five and him declaring that she'd be loosed of the spirit of asthma. The front of Nana's skirt suit jacket soaked with tears as she wobbled back to her seat thanking the Lord for Pastor Ross breathing new life into her that day.

Nana's eyes look like they'll slice my throat if I don't stand up during the last song before the sermon. I stand up, forcing my stank face further down under my skin and scratch at the pantyhose she forced me into just minutes before everybody loaded the van. Tiff was convinced I wouldn't fit none of her clothes, so I ended up back at Nana's to get dressed under her watchful eye. I look fuckin' ridiculous wearing the red spaghetti-strap sundress I packed in case Nana made us dress up. Ridiculous 'cause she made me wear it with a T-shirt and black pantyhose because Nana said I didn't need to be showing all that the Lord gave me in His house. I almost got popped in the mouth trying to remind her that she'd always said the Lord was omnipresent. And don't that mean he's seen it all? Don't that mean he knows it's the only dress I packed?

I scratch at my thigh again as Pastor Ross takes the pulpit for the closing lines of the song. But the musician at the keyboard lingers as they hum for a while and a large projected image of Sandra suddenly appears on the white wall behind him. A picture of her, laughing, at the last family reunion that she, Pop, Fatimah, and I went to as a family. I can't look away from her gap-toothed smile or the press and curl she'd held in place with bobby pins the night before. The deep plum of her lipstick that had made her lips look especially full and sensual even though we always used to hear Nana question how she'd gotten white girl lips, as black as this family is. The way she'd blended some of it into her cheeks with her fingers to add more color to her skin-tagged face. The choir keeps humming, and my eyes move down the blown-up photo to the way her fingertips lightly grazed her collarbone where the Libra pendent she never took off laid. An opal wolf. Thoughtful, selfless. Loyal, balanced. "Libra's hate being alone," she once told me and Fatimah during one of the bedtime stories she'd made up. She pulled us into her perfumed chest and said, "Thas why I'm so glad god blessed me with two of y'all. Mama's babies."

The whole swaying choir is a pixilated blur beyond the tide risen in my bottom eyelids and Pastor Ross's preacher chanting begins. He's saying something about my mama being gone way too soon. That we'd lost another one of the Lord's fallen soldiers. Another beautiful soul. Arms are reaching out to touch me now. To squeeze and shake my shoulders too hard. To tell me it's all right if it hurts and that she's in a much better place now. That she don't have to hurt no more where she is. That I should be strong, hold my head up. I want the hands to go back where they came from. To keep to themselves since they weren't able to keep Sandra alive. To keep her from going sour like forgotten milk in the back of a fridge. Since earth couldn't have been a better place. Since earth rotted her body so much it sent her somewhere that I'll never be able to touch her again. The thought of her becoming too weak to keep breathing makes me collapse back into the pew and let the tears take me under.

Just like my mama, forever below.

What they don't never tell you is how it stops doin' what it s'posed to. How one day it's gon' stop taking away that old feeling. That alive feeling. How it turns you into somebody always trying to get better. Be better. Get back to how you used to be. Everybody starts blaming you. Blaming you for not doing everything right. For not noticing every sign. Every bloody flag. For not being stronger than you was. They gon' make up all types of stories about why this happened to you. Or they might just lie. The truth, too nasty. Too much. Jus' as quick as you came into the world is as quick as they gon' forget what it was like to have you in it. The real you, not the one they thought you was. Who they chose to see. They gon' forget which part of the story they was in. Whether they was the villain or the victim. Everybody loves them a good story. Everybody wanna be sung a good lullaby before they go off to sleep. What if you ain't slept in decades? What if you need something stronger to get there? A little help knowin' what sleep is. What if none of us ever even seen a bed? If you not careful they gon' blame the way you was born. Blame your blood. Blame too many hours looking into the phone waiting for somebody to miss you. To want you. To love you enough to stay.

Just wait. They gon' blame you for it all. Blame you for existing

instead of opening their eyes.

SIXTEEN

The cash-for-houses signs on the way back to Nana's seem like they're everywhere all of a sudden.

I know they weren't just put up last night but today they stick out like neon signs, blinding and pretty much impossible to miss. Some of them are printed in large red lettering against yellow backgrounds, stapled to telephone poles. Others are handwritten in black Sharpie, taped to the glass that covers random bus-stop benches like the person ain't have time to care about what it looked like. Nothing else is on any of the signs, really, besides a phone number they tell you to call if cash for your house is what you want. "We buy houses," but no clue who the *we* is. Guess they figure people around here don't care who they sell they neighborhood to as long as the money looks good. It's hard to believe Nana would ever think her house could be bought by a person who ain't care enough to do more than make one of these basic-ass signs. Or that she'd ever think what they offered was enough.

I let the seat back in Tiff's car, wondering how much white folks would pay for houses in Nana's neighborhood. How little somebody around here might take if they don't know how much they house is really supposed to cost. One time I overheard Pop talkin' to one of his friends on the phone about how high the rent is in Brooklyn and that he'd have to sell his whole life on the street to even think about owning a whole house in New York City. That if word got back to anybody in our family, they'd think he was rolling in cash if he could afford rent that high. By OB standards, they'd think he was rich or something. I count the signs for a while before we turn down Killigans and pull into Nana's driveway. Maleek's sitting on the front porch on FaceTime either using his phone as a mirror, grooming himself, or caking with one of the choir girls who couldn't wait to get home and forget they got saved at the altar for the fifteenth time. Whichever it is, he shuts it down and stuffs his phone in his pocket and folds his hands over his knees. The tips of his locs hang over his legs and look like flecks of fire glowing under the sun pouring over him and Nana's front steps. I get out and walk across Nana's lawn toward him.

"You good?" I know what he's asking and I don't care about answering that question. I don't feel like talking about whatever it was that happened with me at church. He's leaned back on his elbows now, looking around me and down the block as he asks, only making eye contact with me for a few seconds, as if he's waiting on something that ain't me. Or somebody. The white button-down shirt he'd worn to church is untucked and all the buttons, loose, exposing an over-worn, slouching undershirt. When I left the OB, Maleek was a silly boy who couldn't keep his church clothes clean no matter how much of a hawk Nana was. A silly boy who liked to slap his brother across the face, then book it down the hall and out of Nana's before he could get slapped back. Now he looks like a grown man always with someplace important to be and very little time for games. He, like Kobe, was also always ready for anybody tryna throw hands with any of us, but smoother.

"I see you got your lil baby hairs out out! Look at you. A little sun come out and you don't know how to act," I say in response, bringing attention to the small crop of chest hairs he has peeking over the top of his undershirt. To anybody who asks, I'm fine. I'm okay. It's better to just keep it moving. Better to make fun. Maleek follows my lead.

"Shiiiit, it ain't me that don't know how to act. It's all these females that can't resist ya boy. Thirsty as hell and I'ma tall glass of Kool-Aid. The purple kind." My eyes must have rolled all the way to the back of my skull. I see why Kobe can't stand Maleek. He's full of himself and doesn't even try to hide it. When we were kids, it was the church mothers who couldn't resist his charm. Now it's their grandbabies.

"Females or women? It's a lot of things that can be female, cuz. Gotta be more specific. And if you talkin' about women," I say, pausing for a second, "I'm sure the only reason they sweatin' you is 'cause you look a little bit like you got more money than the average OB dude with all that hair on your head and that corny-ass smile." He rolls his eyes over what he'll probably call my big-city language and waves off what I say like an annoying fly that won't stop swarming the food table at a picnic. I've already lost him to his phone again for a good thirty seconds. He's got it back out responding to a text and then leans back again.

All the things filling Nana's porch behind Maleek makes it look like she's prepping for some type of garage sale. Except nobody's ever seen the inside of Nana's garage. At least not none of us kids. A lot of people on another side of town might think it's a bunch of junk, but everything Nana got sitting outside is there for a reason. Just past Maleek's head is the candy cart. To the left of the candy cart is a couch that no longer has the plastic on it because it's too old for the inside of the house but not old enough to be thrown away. To Nana, a couch that ain't covered in plastic isn't fit for her front living room. The one that ain't nobody allowed to sit in. Basically, the part of her house that's a flex—only there to show off and look pretty—even if the rest of the house is chaos. On the other side of the porch is a mini fridge, a porch swing, and a bunch of filled plastic garbage bags. A long time ago I learned the fridge is there for convenience when Nana wants to rest outside, and the swing is there for people who want to see their life flash before their eyes. Sit on it at your own risk. My chest burns when my eyes stop at the plastic bags as Nana's words from yesterday echo in my head.

"You think Nana's packin' already?" I ask, not really wanting to know the answer to that, but still curious. Tiff walks up behind me just in time to hear me.

"Now, you know damn well if Nana was serious she wouldn't be packed till the night before, anyway," she says, trying to make this whole thing another one of her jokes. Maleek grazes his goatee and looks like he's about to say something that he don't wanna say, but Kobe busts through the front door behind him before he can.

"Nana just went in her room. Said she finna rest her eyes for a couple minutes. So that means we got a few hours," he says, speaking directly to Maleek only.

They both tell me and Tiff to come on.

———

Fatimah is separating Robyn's hair into four parts as I come down the stairs. Different-colored beads and barrettes sit next to a huge bottle of pink oil moisturizer on top of the table Robyn winces in front of as the sharp end of the comb drags along her scalp. Her forehead shines under the dim green light, and I can tell she's fighting back tears the way we used to do back when Sandra did me and Fatimah's hair. Robyn looks like she's been popped by the comb a few times like we used to get, too. It's one in the afternoon but the lack of windows down here makes us all forget. Church was three hours long and our bodies can feel it. The whole room feels tired.

"What's she doing here?" is how Fatimah says hello to me. "This ain't nothing that concerns her."

"She's one of us, so she needs to hear this, too. Besides, where else would she go?" Maleek replies. He looks a little sorry for me. Sorry that I've been gone this long.

"Home," Fatimah says without looking up. It stings but for once her and I agree. Home isn't here. Home is where I'm welcome, and all I've felt like since I got here was an unwanted visitor being dragged through muck just for small pieces of happy memories. Somebody who's grown up too much to fit they old clothes. My home is elsewhere. But in this moment, home don't even feel like it's in Brooklyn. Ever since I got on the plane to come back, it feels like I'm still a pigeon, searching. New York City has a way of making you fight to earn your spot in that dump, while Obsidian is a shell of its old nostalgic self, sitting on top of everything you try to forget at the same time.

"I need to hear what?" I ask Maleek, sort of pleading to know what's up. To be treated like I'm wanted here, for real, instead of just guilted for leaving. There's a difference. I sit down on the couch opposite Fatimah and fold my hands looking up at Maleek, ready. Robyn whimpers under the rough pull of her mama's fingers while looking at me and trying to look back at her mom, still looking as curious and confused as the day I walked in Nana's kitchen with her mama's whole face and body. Kobe opens a laptop that he's pulled out of his backpack while Maleek seems to be looking for something on his phone. My phone buzzes in the purse Tiff lent me but whatever's going on in this room right now seems way more important. Tiff finally comes clunking down the steps with a plate, her ear squeezed to her shoulder trying to hold up her phone. Everybody in the room freezes and turns to look at her.

"Uh-huh . . . uh-huh . . . Oh damn, my bad, y'all." She tells whoever's on the other end that she'll call them back and sits between me and my sister. I feel relieved as she digs into the plate Nana had set aside for her. The room is strangely quiet for a few more seconds, and Maleek hands me his phone right before I think I'ma explode. I stare at it for a few seconds confused by what I'm looking at. It's a picture of Nana's house. This house. I study it for a little bit longer trying to crack whatever riddle this is. 'Cause this couldn't be it. No. I squint a little and realize Nana's house don't look like this picture anymore. Now, Nana's house is so . . . old. The one in the picture looks like something somebody would be proud to buy forever ago.

"Okay?" I still don't get what's going on. Kobe sits his computer on my lap.

"This Nana's house on Zillow." It's the same picture of Nana's house from years ago but even newer. And when I look closely, I can tell something's been done to it. Sort of like a digital picture of Nana's house in the future and the listing was posted late last year. In December, just weeks before Sandra died. I try to click the photo like five times quickly, thinking there'd be a whole lot more . . . something a lot more to look at . . . something to explain this to me but there's no other pictures. Not really. Just one other photo that looks like a bird's-eye view of the house from above but with no roof. This one looks even less real and mainly just shows the layout of Nana's house. The inside. Or what it could be. My eyes dart around the page looking for the only thing left for me to see, but my body starts to get too hot for me to think.

"How much is it? Who put this here? When did—"

"Minah." Tiff has her hand pressed gently against my lower back. "Breathe." I try to do what she says while Kobe slowly takes the laptop back from me. "Can y'all hurry the hell up and start talking? You're scaring her." Kobe stands up, rubbing his hands together and pacing the basement floor like a teacher, hype about his lesson while standing in front a roomful of kids who don't even know if they're sitting in the right classroom. I don't even know what grade I'm in. Kobe and Maleek start to tag-team, trying to explain.

"Aight, so. You know what opportunity is, right?" Maleek says like it's a question.

"I look stupid to you?" I say back, tired of feeling like I have to piece things together. He looks back at me like I should relax and then keeps going. For the next ten minutes he and Kobe go back and forth about something called opportunity zones and how Obsidian got tons of them. Nana's house is sitting in one right now. The white folk Nana was talkin' about yesterday are people who want to throw her a little cash so they can take it off her hands, flip it, and then sell it for way more money than they would ever offer her. "Developers" they call them. They go on to tell me that the houses in Nana's neighborhood and other neighborhoods like it in Obsidian—'specially the ones that look abandoned with all the insides on their front lawns—ain't worth much anymore 'cause, at some point, the white folks ain't want them no more. So now they're cheap to buy and when they fix them all up, white folks will wanna live here again. That's when the developers will sell them for more money than any of us ever seen. Or be able to afford. Which means our families would have to find someplace else to live.

"So, that's what's gon' happen to Nana's house? She sold her house to one of those people?" is all I can bring myself to ask.

"Well, they b-b-buyin' up all the houses right now. 'C-c-cause people is moving back to Obsidian. Obsidian is p-p-poppin' right now," Kobe answers. "Y-you seen what downtown look like?" He pauses while I think about Tiff's apartment. The high ceilings. The polished cement floors. The tall windows that had a view of Obsidian River. The wide sidewalks and plastic-looking buildings with bars, galleries, and coffee shops just steps away from the entrance to her apartment. "It ain't always look like that, Minah. It don't look like the river the fam used to kick it at when we was kids. And that's what they tryna do around here. Ain't n-nobody even been able to touch them abandon houses around here. 'Cause they been bought already."

"To turn 'em into condos?"

"Or whatever else they wanna turn our shit into," Maleek adds. "And when they done, it won't be none of us around here no more." A lump the size of a fist, knuckles and all, fills my throat.

"Y'all didn't answer my question," I say, going back to what I asked in the first place. "Is this what's happening to Nana's house? They bought it to sit on it until they ready to turn it into a Starbucks or some shit?" I'm trying my best to speak without them hearing the quiver that's growing in my stomach, making its way up to my chest. I try to silently count in my head and focus on the picture of Nana's house, all new, while I wait for somebody to answer me. Maleek and Kobe just look at each other for a second.

"Not exactly," Maleek says finally. He looks at Kobe again. But this time, a goofy smirk spreading across his face. He sits down across from me and leans in, lowering his voice a little, his eyes flicking once up toward the stairs. "Back when everything was goin' on . . . I called Nana on the phone while me and Kobe was back at the crib. Kobe said I had to do it 'cause, you know . . ." He pauses. Meaning, whatever it was that they were about to do, it couldn't be Kobe because of his stutter.

That would give him away. Kobe been like this forever and everybody act like they can't even say the word or call it what it is. Kobe shoves the bottom of Maleek's chair with the ball of his foot. A nudge to move on. "Anyway, I call Nana up with my white voice. Like that one scruffy-lookin' dude in that movie where he started making all that money from callin' rich folks, selling them slave labor and shit. I tell her that 'I have an amazing offer that she can't refuse.' She ain't know it was me so she kept listening, and I offered her cash like the rest of them. But more than the rest of them. Fatimah told me how much these muh-fuckas had been offering Nana, and I made the number bigger. And told her she won't always have people around to help her up and down the stairs or to take care of her house forever. That time's running out and she needs to start thinking about herself."

"So, y'all the reason Nana's selling our house?!" I say, my voice cracking, tears welling up.

"What you mean *our* house?!" Fatimah cuts, yanking Robyn's braid.

"OW, MOMMY!"

"You been gone someplace else, living large, like you forgot who the fuck you came from and you talkin' about *our*?! Please. You don't even understand what Maleek is saying because, as always, you're only thinking about yourself. Don't worry. Next time you decide to remember who your family is, I'm sure somebody will let you crash on they couch somewhere. I'm sure one of our forgiving cousins will make space for you," she says, finally making eye contact with me.

"We're not the reason," Maleek continues. "But we a better option than what would've happened anyway if we ain't step in. This way we keep what belongs to us."

"Where y'all get the money for this? How y'all got house-buying money?"

"You don't n-n-need to worry about allat, Minah. All you need to know is we takin' care of family business, like we should. Nana won't take our money the normal way so we doin' what we need to do. And we ain't give her all the money yet, anyway. W-w-we just gave her enough so she could tell them white folks that was callin' her every day that they could stop. That she s-sold it to somebody else. That they should l-l-leave her alone. That's givin' us time to get the rest of it."

I don't really have the energy to press for any more details but I ask one last question: "You know you won't be able to trick Nana the whole time. One day she'll want to meet whoever bought her house. What y'all gon' do about that?" The room is already starting to spin. and Nana's always-cold basement feels like it's one thousand degrees.

"We got our ways. Already got the white homie who work at the bank across town to meet up with her once. By the time everything's done, we'll tell her." I pull at the T-shirt under my dress and eventually start to take it all the way off. "She won't be able to do nothin' about it by then."

"Why is it so damn hot in here?" I ask no one specifically.

"Here we go," I hear Fatimah say. But it's muffled, like I've got too much wax built up in my ears.

"You good?" Maleek asks. This time looking more worried about me than he was when we were outside on the porch. I can feel the heaviness of Tiff's hand on my shoulders, gently squeezing. The other rubbing my back. Kobe's using an old magazine to send a breeze toward me, now noticing the sweat that I can't hide from anybody. My body's trembling from the inside, scared of I don't know what. Maybe that everything that I ever knew is changing and it feels like it won't be no way for me to ask my questions. Won't be nowhere for me to go to remember what it was like when things were good.

"What did you mean, earlier," I ask, taking a breath and looking directly at Maleek, "when you said, 'When everything was goin' on'?" This time, unlike the last time we were all here, Maleek uses both hands to pull all the tension through his face and leans forward, ready to answer me.

"When Aunty Sandy was in the hospital, Nana said she ain't know if she'd have the strength to stay on this earth if she lost her baby to—"

"To what?" He looks at Fatimah.

"Listen, Yaminah, Aunty Sandy had got into a little trouble."

"What kind of trouble?"

"Some wild shit. Some shit I don't think we should talk about right now, but she ended up getting hurt. And things ain't go the way it was supposed to." He pauses. "Aunty Sandy was . . . supposed to get better. It wasn't supposed to go down like this. She wasn't supposed to get worse."

She was supposed to live.

SEVENTEEN

"All right, that's it, you got it, Munch! Go'on ahead and step with the other foot right there where you see that groove. You almost there," Pop coaches gently from the ground.

This is the first tree I ever climbed. For Fatimah, it'll be number three. My fingers burn and it feels like all ten of them got little bitty hearts in them, pumping blood. But, looking up, I see Pop's right: almost there. I look down as quick as I can so I don't lose balance and see Fatimah with her arms folded, smiling, like she can't wait to see my face when I fall. Matter of fact, she dares me to do it. "Okay, now grab that little twig right there!" she says. She knows I get nervous when more than one person is talking to me. Fati's death traps are so annoying.

"Shut up, Fati!"

"You shut up and CLIMB!"

"How 'bout everybody shut up so Minah can handle her business," Mama says, her voice getting closer to where I heard Pop's coming from. In three quick steps, I finally get up high enough to sit.

"Finally!" Fati screams, charging toward the bottom of the trunk. "My turn!"

"Now, Crunch—"

"I got it, Pop!" Fati interrupts. And I watch her move up the tree fast like a little squirmy lizard. But with braids.

"Take your time, baby," Mama tells her. Fati's sitting on an opposite branch two minutes later, one bicep in the air flexing for us all to see. "That's my girl! Fast as FloJo!"

"Who's that?!" me and Fati ask at that same time.

"Who is THAT?! Only the fastest black woman in the world! I mean it's been some other girls, but come on now, let's be real. Can you even call yourself fast if you ain't runnin' with six-inch nails on your fingers reminding you that ain't nobody fly as you? Sista was startin' fires on the track," she rambles off to all of us. "And my baby Fatimah gon' be right behind her."

"Yop!" Fati says, co-signing, even though we've never seen the person Mama's talking about. Fatimah has a thing with Mama where Mama gases her up and Fatimah always takes her side in return. Pop pulls Mama closer to him and we know he's about to start up one of his teacher-dad lectures.

"Y'all know what kind of tree this is?" he asks, without pausing long enough to let us guess. "It's a maple tree. They grow all over the world—especially in Asia—but we got 'em right here in Obsidian. Right here in our backyard." All Obsidian parks are our backyard to Pop.

"You mean maple like the syrup you and Mama be puttin' on our pancakes?" Fati asks with her face all scrunched up. I know she's thinkin' what I'm thinkin'. How does that come outta this tree? "Mama be lettin' us make big ol' pancakes when we at Nana house!" she continues, letting go of the branches to show us how big and almost falls. I catch her by the back of her shirt.

"Careful, baby!" Mama says. But Pop moves on with his teacher-dad stuff.

"You know how old this one probably is?" This time he pauses, sizing it up like he can count the years by the lines in the bark. "A little older than y'all, but times THREE!"

"Mama, this tree is thirty like you!"

"AHT! Don't y'all go around tellin' everybody!" she says, fixing her bangs. "If somebody wants to know your mama's age, what y'all gon' say? Like we practiced."

"Twenty-four!" we both scream. Even though twenty-four is just as old as thirty to us. Fatimah's already bored and climbing back down even though Pop said we could only climb the tree if we listened to him going up and coming back down, but Fati probably wasn't listening then, either. Halfway down she jumps and the way she lands, I'm sure she's scraped her knee or something. Everybody freezes while she checks for blood, then hops up running across the grass to another tree. It's like nothing ever really slows Fatimah down and Pop's warnings are just another thing in her way.

"Wait for me!" I start to rush down, trying my best to still listen to how Pop tells me to do it. Behind her, I challenge her to a race. "Bet you can't beat me down there and back here!"

"Bet you I can!" she screams back, already stretching like she's about to dust me. She probably will.

"All right I let this go on for too damn long, y'all need to chill out!" Pop cautions from behind us. The bass in his voice is loud enough to hear every word but not loud enough to be scary. Especially not to Fati.

"Come on, Pop! It's just one race!"

"You sayin' it's just one race now and later we gon' be pullin' your lil ass out the river," he says too fast to stop himself. Pop always goin' off about Fati being reckless. "I mean . . . it's dangerous. Last time—"

"Last time don't count, Pop! You know the ice cream truck song was too loud! Started playing outta nowhere!"

"And what if an ice cream truck come rollin' down the street again, huh?"—putting his fingers up like quotes, raising the pitch of his voice to sound like Fati's—"'Outta nowhere' . . . Whatchu gon' do?"

Fati ignores him and walks over to Mama, leaning in to tell her something we can't hear.

"Me and my baby gon' run our own race over here!" Mama says, shooting a look at Pop. "Relax, John. Always gotta be all serious about everything. Let my baby run." One after the other she pulls each foot up from behind her and hops around a few times in place.

"As long as y'all stay away from the water, I'm cool." Sometimes Pop and Mama sound like they're fighting even when they're saying regular words. I meet Fati and Mama to call the race by the other tree while Pop sits down under the first one Fati chose. Mama kicks off her sandals and the three of us lean out toward the tree we'd just climbed down from. Fati's already giggling.

"Oooon your marks! . . . Get set!! . . . GOOO!!!!" Mama and Fati are both laughing so hard I don't know how they have the energy to run. They pass two people sitting on a blanket together about halfway across the field. And then they start to get close to the turnaround point, still sprinting by each other's side. Pop's standing next to me all of a sudden, his hand resting on my shoulder. He asks me what they're doing and I almost ask him what does it look like? until I notice Fati and Mama are holding hands. Then their feet start to hit the grass at the same time. They're trotting like horses. One, two. One, two. "Hey!" They're not slowing down. They're getting faster. "That's not the finish line! You know you have to run back after you touch it, right?!" I'm screaming at two people who look like they can't hear me or realize the world around them exists.

Like banana skins, the tree in front of them splits open and falls to each side as Mama and Fati start to climb the sky. We never been on a plane before, but this must be what it's like at the airport watching them take off. In each of their free hands appear red balloons like they're on their way to god's birthday party. "Wait, what are y'all . . ." They're going too high. Running behind them, I look to my side to ask Pop how we're gonna get them back down. But when I look, Pop's too far behind. "This is all your fault," I scream to him. "How am I supposed to do this without you?" Like he's frozen in time, his body gets smaller and smaller. Then his voice hums close to my ear as I reach the tree's bottom, stretched upright again as if nothing ever happened:

"Forgive me," Pop says. "Forgive me . . ."

———

What's worse?

Sandra dying or her coming back every time I close my eyes?

OUSE

EIGHTEEN

The street is almost completely silent once Tiff pulls the keys out the ignition.

Tiff, Kobe, and I just sit here, breathin' in one another's air while I get myself together enough to step out the car. I told Kobe I wanted to come here, but to be honest, I wasn't all the way sure about what I was askin' or what it is that I came to find. It don't even look like the street we grew up on no more and don't nobody live anywhere close enough for us to see. By the way it looks, this couldn't be the same place with the most perfect grass where me and Fatimah used to roll all over the front lawn tryna pin each other down. Or the place where Pop built our own personal sandbox in the backyard. Couldn't be the same place where he also planted rosebushes that died and came to life every spring like couldn't nothin' keep them from blooming like they were supposed to. Couldn't be this place. And if it is, I need to see it for myself, up close.

Tiff pops the trunk, and Kobe walks around to fish out the crowbar. She grabs a flashlight the size of her head and pulls a bat from underneath a flap. I stare at her for a minute, and she looks back at me like I couldn't be so stupid not to know what she's carrying it for. The plywood boards nailed all over the house look rotten. It's the first thing I smell, damp and sour, suffocating every opening that me and Fati used to hang our legs out on the days it got too hot and the AC was broken. Sandra would call us over to the side of the house, claiming she needed help with Pop's rosebushes, then she'd turn the hose on us. She'd chase us around the corner to the front with us screaming between the laughing that took the wind out of us until we could make it inside. We'd take our soaked clothes off right at the door and put our backs upside down on the couch in front of the living room window to let our feet catch the breeze. She'd come in a few minutes later, shaking her head at us and say, "Silly babies. So damn gullible." I didn't know she was calling us easy to trick. Too easy to fool. Sandra wasn't the gardening type, and we should have known. She fooled us all.

Kobe stops at the top step of the front porch as I pass him by, studying where the front door used to be.

"All you came here to do was look at the door?"

"What door? How we supposed to get in when it ain't no real doors or windows around here?" I ask him, turning around to look him in the eye. He peers back at me like it's the dumbest thing he ever heard.

"What you mean? Same way you get in if there was doors and windows and they was locked. Plywood ain't nothin." He takes two steps over and jams the crowbar into the house, hooking in onto the top edge of plywood covering me and Fati's favorite window. He yanks hard, pulling it out at the first try. Surprisingly, most of the glass is still there, hanging on like a kid with a mouthful of blood losing a fight, just waiting to have the rest of their teeth knocked out. Kobe clears all the glass around the window's edge and stands to the side to let me climb in first. Foolishly expecting our couch to still be where it was, my body crashes onto the dusty floor below.

———

You know the creepy house on the end of the deserted block that all the grown folks in movies tell kids to stay the hell away from? The one that ain't nobody been in for years 'cause it's haunted by a clown that hangs out in gutters waiting to kill us or something? It feels like that's our house now. And it's weird to say that 'cause the last time I saw it, it felt like the safest place I'd ever been.

I broke the fall with my arm and it takes a minute of me rotating my shoulder after I stand up to notice I'm covered in cobwebs, thick dust, and a little bit of glass. Tiff coughs behind me and I jump. I don't wait for either of them to climb through before I dart toward the stairs, headed up to me and Fati's room, my legs skipping every other stair like my body remembers doing every day after school.

"Minah, be—" I hear Tiff yell behind me before her voice is drowned out by the pitch blackness of the second floor, and the shock of it nearly blows me back down the stairs. I don't know why I expected light. All three doors that I imagined being open are closed, and it feels like the dark's fingers are crawling all over me. I quickly push the bathroom door open to let the skylight's brightness pour in so I can see something, and the wood creaks under my first step. Someone's yanked up every tile. But a small cup sits next to the sink and the faucet gurgles a bit before gushing out orange water when I turn one of the knobs. A roach crawls out the drain at full speed and I hear Sandra callin' it a water bug in my head while I jump back. "Y'all think that little-ass bug gon' do somethin' to you?" she'd ask us after we'd come running from wherever we saw one. We'd tell her how it ran toward us and not away, and she'd just laugh before scooping it up with paper and opening the front door to set it free. Sandra was the only black person I knew who wouldn't even kill a cockroach. Well, besides Fatimah. She was scared but would rather see it live. "That thang is more scared of you than you're scared of it. And jus' 'cause you scared don't mean it deserves to die," she'd say, looking at me, closing the door behind her. We'd still squirmed and ran back up the stairs screaming until whatever game we'd made up that day made us forget what we'd seen.

Me and Fati's bedroom was the stereotypical stuff of two little girls' dreams. A bunk bed with matching *Dora the Explorer* covers. White Christmas lights braided into the ladder up from my bed to Fati's. All the walls covered in my watercolor paintings and Fati's magazine-collage experiments. A small desk in front of the window with more cups of paintbrushes, colored pencils, and markers than we needed. Above the desk, Poopie the Parakeet would sit perched in his gold birdcage, sometimes singing a song Sandra taught him, and across the room a small TV sat on top of an overstuffed toy chest, bursting with every kind of black Barbie doll that Pop could find us. The TV was old and only used for two things: *George of the Jungle* on Saturday mornings and reruns of *American Idol* on Friday nights. Me and Fati would pull our comforters off our beds and make a futon out of them for our parents to sit on. Sandra never missed a chance to remind us that she could out-sing every last one of those blubbering so-called singers, and in another life, she would have dusted light-skinned Jordin Sparks. She was feeling herself getting older, constantly reminding us that nothing was as it used to be and these baby-faced singers, as she called them, didn't know nothin' about real entertainment like the ones that came out of Michigan back in the day. That they take their freedom for granted, standing in one spot for a whole song when they got a whole stage to move across and bodies that ain't never seen the work of pushing out two babies on the same day. Then she'd cough, spit into her empty wineglass, and go outside for a "walk" during the commercial breaks.

The emptiness of the room echoes back at me when I push our old bedroom door closed. I light up an American Spirit and sit all the way down, cross-legged, in the middle of it, leaning back on one hand to let my head hang for a second. I look over and watch a pregnant spider crawl across the window's edge and exhale the smoke in its direction. We learned how to spot a pregnant spider the day Pop killed one while Sandra was out. It looked fatter than all the other ones we'd seen, so I begged Pop to kill it. Fati thought it was kind of cool, but it was in our bedroom and I knew there wasn't no way I'd be able to sleep at night knowing it was crawling all over the place in there. It was just too big. A whole monster. He smashed it with his house shoe and it looked like at least one thousand babies came running out in every direction as fast as they could away from their dead mother. Fati ran across the hall and barely made it to the bathroom toilet in time while I sat there on my knees unable to move or even look away. The hallway suddenly stank of sour peanut butter, rancid strawberry jelly, and yeasty white bread from our after-school snack. I didn't eat another PB&J for years after that. I'd just begged Pop to kill somebody's mama. Even after Pop had shown us their life cycle in a book at the library a few weeks later, it still hadn't been enough for Fati. Even after he'd told us spider babies can fend for themselves without their mama right after being born, it took her a long time to forgive us. She said I should have just let her take it outside, given it a chance. That we couldn't just get rid of things because we're scared. We borrowed the book from the library that day and, later, studied how to tell if a spider was pregnant: a bigger-than-normal belly and a white sac being made in its web somewhere nearby, it said.

I barely hear the door open before Tiff is sitting down next to me on the thick dust blanket that I'm trying not to think too much about

in the middle of my old room. She slides two fingers around my cigarette to lift it from my hand to her mouth. Inch-long ash falls to the
floor around her Sha'Carri Richardson–inspired acrylics, like confetti
at the end of a race. Tiff might spend all her work hours in music spots
surrounded by rich white boys who sag their khaki cargo shorts and
wear their baseball caps backward to downplay their privilege, but she
will never be too good to pay homage to ghetto creativity. She's been
doing the most with her nails ever since she was old enough to pay
for them with her hard-earned babysitting money. Before the night-
life gigs, she used to be Nana's backup when the number of random
kids being dropped off on her porch became too much. Tiff's parents
weren't the type to stand in the way as long as she pulled her own
weight, and that meant making enough to pay for things she didn't
need. Outside of food and shelter, that was pretty much everything.

"Yo. Y'all's sleepovers used to be the best," she says, gazing around
the room with deep nostalgia in her eyes. "Your mama ain't care what
we watched like err'body else's mama." Both of our mothers became
too busy around the same time. My house had all the snacks, and
meeting me and Fatimah was like getting two play cousins for the
price of one.

"And look how great y'all turned out." Kobe's grown-man voice is
ice water on my back even after being here for almost five days.

In the fifth grade me and Fati discovered why the school's computers was always blocking us from most of the internet. There were
weird videos that didn't seem to belong to any regular TV station, and
it wasn't nothing we'd ever seen in the movies. According to Sandra,
we weren't old enough to have our own phones, but Tiffany had managed to get her hands on one. Then one day she showed us what her
phone started doing after she accidentally clicked some commercial

that popped up on Google and then a whole bunch of other videos started popping up randomly. And they were all sort of the same: a few minutes of bad acting and awkwardness and then suddenly we'd hear moans, skins slapping, and see moving naked flesh across the screen. The first time a full scene began playing on Tiff's phone, me and Fati ran screaming down Nana's block, laughing until we snorted. The second time was the beginning of Tiff coming over every weekend when Sandra started going out almost every night. With saliva-stained pillows, worn blankets, and funky wrinkled sheets we turned our bunk beds into the fort of our dreams and kept the volume extra low, watching each scene, searching with our ears tuned for Pop appearing outside the door. We were ten going on eleven, and we had questions, but our mamas were somewhere else.

I turn toward Kobe to see him looking down at me again, while bending slightly to lift the cigarette out of Tiff's hand so he could bring it up to his mouth. "Can't believe you be smoking this shit, too," he says on the exhale. Kobe does everything like he's been doing it his whole life. Like he was never taught anything by anyone; he just came out his mama experienced and sick of life already. He takes another pull and hands my cigarette back to Tiffany like he knows what's best for me and that it's his job to keep me from getting any worse.

"I don't. I look like a smoker to you?" I'm not lying. My mom's dead, and I'm back in the house where everything changed. Who is Kobe to judge me? People who smoke smell like Newports and always gotta spit. Smokers know the consequences of their actions and do it anyway. Smokers party instead of handling their problems for real. I'm not a smoker. I can stop whenever I want.

I feel Tiff and Kobe stare at each other even though I've turned away.

The way Pop used to look at Kobe and Maleek made me feel the same way I felt about going anywhere near Sandra and Pop's bed: could be fun but likely dangerous. An adventure that was marked from the beginning, built in a way that's naturally destined for disaster no matter how careful. Sharp things always find their way to whatever's easiest to prick. When Pop told us him and Sandra were getting a waterbed, my brain panicked thinking of our house becoming an aquarium and how all the times I'd gone to the one downtown with Pop and Fati, the furthest thing from my mind was sleep. Water is a place where you drown even when you're careful. A flood always starts with a leak. Pop looked at Kobe and Maleek like unfastened safety pins carelessly left to fall between the bed frames just under a mattress full of water, likely to ruin everything, especially their own lives. In Pop's eyes there was a long list of reasons to stay away from my cousins, who he claimed were always out doin' things they had no business doin'. I was to stay focused and keep my distance if I didn't want to be caught in a flood.

Unlike the bed, the rest of Pop and Sandra's old bedroom is mostly left like it was the last time I saw it: A king-sized bed frame—dark wood and leather—still holding a water mattress that's now drained, my recurring childhood nightmare disarmed. A sour stench rising from the old carpet and steaming off the walls. Random things like telephone cords, business cards, and lotion bottles are spilling out of both nightstands on the sides of the bed frame. Sandra's dried-up nail polish bottles and perfumes are scattered all over their dresser. I hear a slow, rhythmic drip coming from the tub in their private bathroom and walk in to see rust climbing up from the drain and along the tub walls where Fati and I used to take our bubble baths most nights before bed. The way me and Pop left this house four years ago confuses me. Is this is how he left their room, taking nothing with him? Leaving everything in its place with no pressure on him to pack the way I had to? He left so much behind while forcing me to carry memories of Sandra and Fati with me whether I wanted to or not. I never knew I could just check out like grown folks do. I wasn't the first one to leave everything behind.

The walk-in closet was like a forbidden place full of things little girls should never touch with their sticky, candied hands, but me and Fati always looked at it like our personal circus tent when our parents weren't around. And now with nothing in it but a few of Pop's old shirts, sullied and stomped on by work boots, I can't resist the urge to play inside it. My body is a star, mid-cartwheel, moving from one side to the other when I hear glass break downstairs, followed by boots crunching over the new mess. Kobe and I almost knock each other down like bowling pins racing downstairs toward the sound, but it's me who gets close enough to see the person first. A camera flashes at least seven times before the person behind it lowers a Nikon away from her face and glances at both of us like we need to wait our turn. She talks to us anyway.

"This place is sick. To me, it's even more epic than all the others. People think those abandoned warehouses covered in graffiti—like the shit you see in movies about New York City?—are the coolest to explore, but that's so typical. Me?" she says, answering and asking questions I never had for her. She takes a step closer to what's left of our two-door refrigerator and crouches down to get a shot from below. "Me, I like vintage. That old-school Obsidian look with the pastel-colored tiles everywhere, sunrooms, and abstract stained-glass windows. Some of them still have the cabinets where they kept the fine china that I'm sure nobody ate off of."

I don't like the way she says nobody. I don't like how she drags out the *no* part like anything luxurious is obviously beyond anyone who's ever lived around here. She laughs and looks around the kitchen, taking steps in a circle as she straightens her back. She's a kid at an amusement park, making plans to go on all the rides and eat up everything her hands can touch. "You can almost smell the homecooked meals that used to stink up these walls. Like real hardworking folks used to live here with their families."

"That's because they did" is all I can push out through clenched teeth. Both fists become an Arthur meme, tightened at my sides.

"I'm Marin." She steps toward me with an extended hand in the same moment that Kobe comes from around me to block her.

"Do it look like we care about your name?"

"Look, I—"

"This what you do? Go around breaking into people's houses?"

"Nobody li—"

"Wrong." Now Kobe's fully standing in front of me, his body casting a cool shadow over my face and Tiff. Kobe's back muscles press against the inside of his T-shirt and I trace their movement down his biceps along the bulging veins that lead me to his tightened fists. I don't know where he found it, but this is when I notice one of his fists is wrapped around a piece of wood that's as long as his arm. I envy him for being prepared to do what I've already imagined doing to this stranger. We both take a step toward Marin and I take another to the side. Marin's eyes dart to the plank, then past both of us toward Tiff's hand. The bat.

"Kobe—" I whisper.

Marin looks down at the plank, eyes wider than when she was looking at our house like a secret treasure she'd soon cash in on.

"I don't put my hands on women, so you can relax." He takes another step closer to her so he's within inches of her face. "But you need to get on up out of here. I don't never see nobody like you around here unless they got a camera or a notebook in they hand. Looks like you're in uniform," he says, nodding toward the camera she's finally stopped using. Marin's hands are visibly shaking as she backs away from Kobe and climbs back out the same window she came in from. She keeps her eyes locked on us until she's fully outside.

Then she runs.

NINETEEN

I don't remember much after Kobe's threat and Marin run-
ning like she might, for once, actually be penalized for taking something that wasn't hers. But there was lots of crashing and flying nails.

Lots of loose plywood left on the front porch. My own blood everywhere and all I can feel now is the breeze slapping my face coming in
from the passenger-side window, Tiff's car bouncing me around in my
seat at every pothole and red light. When I close my eyes every few
seconds, two figures sit at the bottom of the stairs watching me. Kobe's
voice tells me that it's okay. That the white girl is gone now. That this is
still my house and that we can get it back. That he'll find a way. Every so
often my small arms knock something else down that's twice my size.
My sneakers crunch over the small, broken pieces of my childhood. I
open my eyes and let a small river run out and then shut them again to
see myself retrieving my fist from a wall, marveling at the hole it's left
behind. On the porch, my body swings back and forth like a kid flying
from one monkey bar to the next, my hands attacking another wall
with my fingers clenched around some plywood's edge until the nails
tear loose. It sends me stumbling back and I do it again. And again.
And again until that isn't enough. I open my eyes again and let the
river continue and then I shut them one more time to see me flying
off the porch stairs, stomping and kicking at whatever's in my way and
I don't stop until I reach the car.

TWENTY

"It's gon' have to be a few more days, Munch."

"But you said to call you when I'm ready," I tell Pop, my voice cracking in the way that makes me feel like Sandra's broken me, even six feet beneath us. I don't like sounding like an abandoned puppy, whimpering to be let back inside while its owner lies dead on the other side of the door.

"I know, I know. And I'll book your flight as soon as I can, but money's a little tight over here. I need to work some things out. You gonna have to hold on tight for a little bit while I figure things out, okay?" There's probably nothing more awkward than crying on FaceTime, but that's what I did so Pop could see how miserable I am. I want him to feel bad for sending me here, then leaving me to be ripped apart. "Come on, Munch. It can't be that bad. You're with family." The word *family* fills Pop's mouth like scrambled eggs, too hot and mushy, burning his tongue and falling back out onto the plate like a bite taken way too soon. Me and Pop are a family all on our own back in Crown Heights. We were making a life for ourselves far from what used to be before someone had to come and remind me that that "family" used to include four of us.

"Yeah, well, I gotta go."

When we moved to Brooklyn, I thought I'd never be able to sleep, with constant sirens, car horns, and soca music piercing the air all night, but nothing really holds a torch to the sound of crickets. I used to think there'd be no way I could call a place home if I was always having to watch my back for pickpockets on crowded subway trains and angry, cursing drivers on the street. I felt there was no way I could get used to being thousands of miles away from all that I'd ever known. And then, soon after, all that I'd ever known became so far in the background that it didn't feel like pretend when I started creating a new me. Someone who didn't eat things that came from animals anymore and who believed in the stars instead of some vengeful, invisible god. Someone who lived in a big city where nothing ever really closed and everybody's life was hard and no one gave a fuck about a girl without a mother she could talk to. In Brooklyn, everyone had a hard story, so who cared about mine? Who cared that anyone had been mean to me or that my mama had changed almost overnight? In New York, that was every day and so I just decided I'd leave it all behind, just like Pop had done with all the stuff him and Sandra shared. He left it all behind like it never even happened. And if it never happened, then we aren't so broken, are we?

It's nowhere near dark outside yet but the crickets behind Nana's house are going off so I couldn't sleep the rest of this day away even if I tried. Pop used to call this time of day prime time for catching lightning bugs.

In the scary third-floor bathroom the cold tile is shocking but feels better than all my other feelings, and I pull the tie out of my hair, letting my twists fall over my shoulders. Mike always says he loves seeing me this way. Says it's nice feeling like he gets to see a side of me that I barely ever let the rest of the world know exists. The phone only rings once before Mike's face fills the screen. If the big creepy-eyes emoji were a person . . .

"Damn, boo, what's ya name?"

"Yaminah," I say, playing along, pretending to be a shy girl he's just trying to talk to on the street. I prop the phone up against the sink mirror so he can see more of me and start loosening a twist.

"Where you from, Yaminah? I know you not from the Bronx 'cause I ain't seen nobody like you around." He's fully cheesing into the screen now, not even trying to hide that his eyes are searching my whole body. He once told me it didn't matter that I was always wearing oversized T-shirts. He's got a great imagination and, sometimes, X-ray vision, he said. Plus, "it's always the shorties in the baggy clothes that be the baddest." Mike's game was average, at best, but he became my boyfriend because he always seemed to be telling the truth. At least the truth the way he saw it.

"Obsidian," I say, visibly surprising myself. Saying it and seeing Mike's face at the same time reminds me that I'm still trapped here and I pick up my phone, opening my texts, to try one last thing.

"Obsidian? Where's that at? I don't know nobody from Obsidian. Prolly why you so different, huh?" He's trying to keep our role play going, but I've already quit. A text back from Tiff pops up across the top of the screen: *sorry cuz. i need all my coin. you hate being here that bad? damn i thought you missed us.* I reach the root of my first twist and pull the loosened extension from my scalp, revealing a thick coil of my own hair. I scratch my scalp and drop the fake hair into the sink, looking at myself in the mirror. Sandra would want no part of this natural hair mess. It would probably be enough that I didn't wear any makeup or get my nails done like Fati had started asking to do when we were kids. But not relaxing my hair, running around here with so much shrinkage after I washed that I looked like a little boy? That's where she'd draw the line. She'd faithfully worn wigs almost every day the last time I'd seen her but that was besides the point. Nobody in Obsidian wore their hair natural, and walking around like an African booty-scratcher ain't how you catch one. Not if you wanted one who had money. Sandra took to teaching me and Fati how to catch a man with money right before she stopped coming home altogether. Why didn't I tell Mike I was from Brooklyn like all the other times? "Talk to me, babe. I mean, I could watch you take down ya twists all day but we ain't talked in a minute."

"But I don't want to talk about me. Tell me a story." I've moved onto the next twist but pause, placing my hands on the cold sink. I let my head drop back and take a deep breath in to make sure not a single tear drops. "Please?"

Mike is quiet for a few moments and then I watch him walk back into the kitchen from the bathroom, remove his apron, and tell the manager that he's taking his break. Outside, he takes a long walk through Bed-Stuy telling me about the time he got trapped inside one of the train cars with a New York City rat. By the time he gets to the end of the story, I'm laughing so hard my belly hurts and I'm halfway through taking down my hair. Mike gets quiet for a while and I know he's waiting for me to tell him something. "Even with all those big-ass rats, I rather be there than here," I finally tell him.

"It's that bad?" He's now walking back toward the restaurant.

"I mean, I got to kick it with my cousins and all that, but everything here is still the same as it used to be. The same ol' shit as when I was growing up. Ain't nobody doing anything or going anywhere out here. Well, except maybe Tiff. She got a job working concerts and stuff like that downtown. And you wouldn't believe her apartment. It's the only cool thing I've seen since I been here." I take my eyes off the phone for a while, making eye contact with my reflection moving my hands to the back of my head, my arms starting to ache as I loosen the last few twists. I hear myself rambling about the reunion and church and Nana's house for a while before I notice Mike hasn't said anything for at least a full five minutes. "You there?"

"Yeah."

"Why you not sayin' nothin', then?" It feels like way too much time passes before he says anything, and large chunks of my hair stick out in all directions as if stretching itself toward all corners of the bathroom, my voice echoing across the entire third floor. I scratch my head, feeling self-conscious all of a sudden, realizing Mike's seeing me naked sort of. I don't even look like me to myself. Mike's face twists in a way that I don't understand. "What is it?"

"Yo." For a minute, getting his words out looks as hard as tying a cherry stem into a knot with your tongue. At least I've never been able to do it. "You talkin' like those ain't your peoples," he says. "Like that ain't where you really from. You been gone for how long? And they let you come back?"

He doesn't understand.

"Aye, I gotta clock back in. I'll holla at you later." And he hangs up the phone.

———

The test was mostly like Ms. Dunham said it would be. And worse.

How was I supposed to know the whole shit was basically going to be about dying? The whole time we were learning Living Sciences it never once made me think it was gon' be all about our parents and passing things down before all of us stop existing eventually. Nikki tried to help me. Tried to get me to study. Tried to make studying fun. Even told Mike to back off a little so I'd have enough time to prepare

myself for this exam that don't nobody outside of New York even have
to worry about, but nothing really worked. There was no way anything
could prepare me for that kind of attack. In school. In front of everybody.

The transfer of genes from parents to their offspring is known as
(a) differentiation
(b) heredity
(c) immunity
(d) evolution

I understood the question and I knew the answer but circling it
would mean that whatever happened to Sandra could happen to me.
Probably would happen to me. And she isn't here for me to ask her
how it happened or what it was like. On Sunday in church the pastor
called out the demon of stomach cancer and bound it in the name of
Jesus. Said that demonic spirit of sickness has no place in this family,
and all I wondered was why somebody hadn't made sure of it before
it took my mama? What use was God if He was always too late? What
was God's obsession with sacrifice? First, His only son, and then, my
only mama? Fuck God, then. Fuck a god who would take the first home
I ever had. I wasn't speaking to her before she died, but it wasn't up to
anyone else to decide the rest of our relationship for me. Nikki didn't
understand how I could be so smart and still end up having to do final
exhibitions over again. She said she knew I was sad and all, but that
she and I had already studied before I even knew. No one understands
what happens to you when your mama dies. Nobody understands anything that's never happened to them. They don't know this is the worst
thing that's ever happened to you in your entire life. Deep down they

wish you would just get over it so you could stop acting all different. Little things they do tell you they wish you would just go back to being fun again. I mean, Nikki ain't everybody secretly wishing I would stop being weird, but I know she feels it a little. Even though she tries not to show it.

Back in Sandra's old room I find a floral scarf that looks like it's lived on way too many heads, thick with grease, draped over the dresser. I wrap my dirty hair with it before I open both closet doors, pull open every drawer, and kneel to look under the bed when I don't yet find anything I feel like snooping through. Dust and funk shoot up my nose and I sneeze so hard I'm dizzy for a second, wiping whatever comes out on the back of my hand. Under Sandra's old bed is a shoebox marked with the word HAPPY. I slide it out and sit back on my feet.

Unlike Pop, Mama kept everything. Inside the box there are receipts with song lyrics written down the back, bent-up drive-in movie stubs, and numbers written on a white flashcard she'd safety-pinned to her chest at auditions. Black-and-yellow playbills, a set of eyelashes, and an almost fully used stick of deep purple lipstick, dried up and useless. Under those, handwritten love notes from Pop, birthday cards, and a corsage decorated in pink, purple, and blue flowers. At the bottom, stick-figure drawings created with every color crayon from me and Fati, next to our birth certificates folded in half. FATIMAH OKAR: *May 11, 2003. 9:17 a.m.* YAMINAH OKAR: *May 11, 2003. 9:24 a.m.* Mama couldn't get Fatimah to shut up about being older than me once she found out, even though we were the same exact height, weight, and celebrated being born on the same day every year. It didn't matter. Knowing she was born seven minutes before me, no matter how much of a reflection of each other we were, Fati always reminded me she was the older sister and that I better quit acting like I'm better than her or something.

I fold the certificate with my name on it in half and slide it into my backpack before I find the large envelope at the bottom of the box marked DON'T BEND. In it is a photo of Mama and Pop on their wedding day, smiling so hard it looks like their cheeks must have hurt, but they didn't seem to care. Mama's dress looked like something I've seen white girls wear to prom in eighties movies, and Pop's tux looked like he was dressed for somebody's funeral, minus the lavender-colored bow tie he wore to match the flowers pinned into Mama's wig. Mama threw a full vase with water and roses still in it at Pop the day she moved out. Me and Fati heard the glass breaking, and Pop later tried to tell us it was an accident. That he'd knocked it off a table with his elbow, but we could hear Mama's voice through the floorboards, her cadence sounding like it lurched from someone else's body. She'd stomped up the stairs and into their bedroom like she was in a rush, where we watched her run around throwing clothes into a small suitcase, violently cursing under her breath. She was a tornado sweeping up random trash cans and cars in its path. The whole house shook when she slammed the door behind her. We peeked through the blinds of our bedroom window, watching her jog to the curb to hop in the passenger seat of a car we'd never seen before. Briefly, her eyes had flicked up toward us like she only had the energy to think the word *goodbye*. No use saying it.

Under the hot shower, I sit all the way down on the tub floor combing out chunks of conditioner-soaked hair from the roots to the ends just like Sandra taught me. Carefully, I pull the comb through my coils the way she said you should do it so you don't lose too much hair. Every few strokes, I pause to look at the clump of dead strands built up in it and wonder if doing it like this still helped Sandra at all when she started losing her hair. That's what I heard chemo does to people with cancer, but I've never seen a black woman with cancer on TV. Black women shaved their heads and went wig shopping with their families to hide the way their bodies stopped working. Mama already wore wigs for all the different women she wanted to be. She had multiple for different occasions but kept her hair cut as short as Pop's under them because she didn't have time to be fussing about no hair. Sometimes they even went to the barbershop together if she didn't feel like being in Nana's basement. Still, she said she was a lady and would never let anyone see her looking like she ain't belong to nobody. So much better to let everybody see you angry than anybody see you lookin' all sad.

TWENTY-ONE

The worst sound in the world is the sound of somebody chewing their food.

It gets worse when the person chews with they mouth open or smacks because they don't bother to wait till they're finished to start talking to you. Multiply that terrible sound by one million if you're sitting at a table surrounded by a bunch of impatient loudmouths and you get Nana's dining room table by six o'clock. Hands are everywhere reaching for extra slices of white bread, another shake of hot sauce, and handfuls of limp thick-cut fries. At the center of the table sits a tall mound of catfish fried perfectly like every other time we'd gone over Nana's for dinner. Nana has never missed. Earlier she'd said the secret is buttermilk.

"Most people don't bother to take they time with the fish like it deserves," she said, slightly leaned over the stove, gently lowering the last few pieces into the bubbling Crisco with her bare hands. "They think some egg batter and a little flour is enough, the way they fry they chicken. Amateurs." Nana's catfish frying is a whole process that Sandra had never passed down. Pop was more of the chef than her, but I remember her still being serious about the texture. Lightly crisp and golden brown on the outside, juicy, flaky on the inside or she didn't want it. "The buttermilk goes into the egg batter, then you season it. Then you put it in your cornmeal and make sure it's covered all the way. You season that, too. And it don't need to be in the oil for long or you gon' have some fish-flavored mashed potatoes and don't nobody want that nasty mess." She paused and chuckled to herself, like she was talking from experience but an experience that was from the before times when old folks were still kids. As if shaking whatever memory that was away, she blinked her eyes a few times before placing one hand on her hip and using the other to break a piece off a filet that's done to hand it to me. "Go'on and taste that miracle," she tells me, not caring that I've told her I'm vegan now at least three separate times. And right now I don't care either. All of us inhale Nana's version of heaven like we'll never get a chance to eat again while she sits on the back stoop smoking under the hot summer sky. I mostly eat in silence, still feeling like a guest without Tiff, Kobe, or Maleek around. I eat fast so I can wash my plate and sit next to Nana outside.

"What you gon' do with that mop on yo' head?" She hasn't even looked at me yet so she must have had that question waiting since before dinner. "You want me to call your Aunty Jo?"

"I'm good, Nana. I like my hair" is all I say at first, watching the smoke float up and disappear into the starless sky. Gazing up at its emptiness is strangely peaceful until I'm reminded of how easy it was for Nana to let all of this go. Back when Fati and I were in kindergarten, we were convinced it wasn't just the house Nana owned; she owned everything we could see from it, too. "Why you don't want your house no more, Grandma?"

Nana doesn't say anything for a long time, pulling hard on her cigarette a few more times before smushing it under her rubber house shoe. Today's she's dressed head to toe in lavender with a blond bob pulled over her stocking wig cap.

"How you doin' up there on the third floor?" she asks.

"I guess I'm fine."

"You lie just like yo' mama. I know the third floor is a hot mess. Probably funky as hell."

"I don't—"

"You know why it's like that up there, chil'? 'Cause ain't nobody tryna climb up three flights of stairs at seventy-eight."

This is the first time I've ever heard Nana's age. Guess if anybody ever asked me how old my granny is, I would have just said old.

"That's why. Y'all kids come and go through yo' granny's house as you please and don't have no idea what it takes to keep this place from falling apart. I'm tired. What I need a big ol' house like this for all by myself?"

I let my eyes float above Nana's head to the baby-blue-colored paint peeling along the edges of the door behind us. Looking closer, I can tell this house has been two other colors before this and realize I never really thought that much about Nana's house that deeply. Guess Nana's house was just Nana's House to me. Almost like family, it's just always been, and in my head, it would forever be.

"What about all those kids that live here, Nana? Where they gon' go?"

"Don't none of those babies belong to me. They parents just know I'll feed them, and with me, they safe. I don't turn no hungry children away and they parents is out working three and four jobs just to keep up with rent around here. Only reason I ain't been kicked out yet is 'cause this house is mine and I say when I get to go. I'm leaving now because I'm good and ready." She pushes her fingers into my freshly washed 'fro and rubs my scalp before grabbing a chunk of hair to squeeze. "My Lord, this thang is worse than a Brillo pad." Something shuffles around in Nana's garage and both of us freeze, looking toward it.

"You think somebody's in there, Nana?"

"Probably ain't nothin' but a raccoon. It'll take care of itself. All that noise it's makin' snoopin' around in there most likely already scared it away. And if it don't, it'll leave when it don't find what it's lookin' for."

"What's that Nana?"

"Uh, food?" she says back, shaking her head, like it's a question even though it's the answer. "And here I was thinkin' you were the smart one. Ain't got no baby or boys distracting you and still gon' ask me what a raccoon is looking for." Nana don't have to say much more for me to know she's comparing me with Fatimah like everybody else has always done since the day we were born. I haven't had to be back that long to notice the whispers and the side comments about which one of the twins is the embarrassment and which one is the family prize, worthy of all the gold stars. Even though everybody around here seems to have an attitude about how long I been gone, they still make it clear that I'm the twin who still has a chance to make something of myself while Fatimah can only get but so far here in Obsidian as a sixteen-year-old mom. Nana stands up and starts to shuffle up the driveway, searching the perimeter of the house for weeds to pull. With nothing else to do, I follow her. "You ain't mess with no boys yet, is you?"

Nana pauses and looks me up and down like it's probably unlikely, judging by the way that I dress. It's always made me feel so weird how family works. You could do months, maybe years, without seeing somebody, and just because they're your relative, they could have the right to ask you anything they want about your personal life and you're expected to answer. Nikki's always talking about boundaries and "me time" and telling her mom no when she doesn't want to do something or doesn't want her to go in her room, but that's completely foreign in this family. Seems like ain't no such thing as privacy or boundaries with this family. We could go in and out of each other's lives and still act like we have a right to whatever information we want. Or at least that's how the grown folks around here act. Just because they were around when I was born, they believe they still know me and that alone means I still owe them in some way. I think about lying to Nana about Mike but then I decide it doesn't matter. She wouldn't even be able to do anything about the truth. "I have a boyfriend, Nana."

"A boyfriend? What you know about having a boyfriend?" She pulls up a bunch of dandelions near the steps of the back patio.

"I know enough."

"Well, excuse me. I ain't know you was grown." Adults always take everything to the extreme when you show just a little bit of confidence in a choice you made just because when they were your age, they fucked it up. "Your mama thought she was grown, too. That's how she . . . well, anyway." Nana's voice trails off as if she's suddenly entered a daydream. She moves the dandelion stems around in her hands as if trying to bring herself back down from wherever she came from.

"What happened to my mama, Nana?"

"Your mama wasn't like anybody else in Obsidian, baby."

"What do you mean?"

"She felt things. She felt things way more than most of us. More deeply. And I guess those feelings just swallowed her up. Got tired of fighting and gave up." Now with both hands full she drops the dandelions into the backyard trash can and dusts her hands off on her jean skirt before lighting another cigarette. The almost-empty pack of American Spirits throbs against the inside of my pocket and my fingers itch, resisting the urge to pull one out, too. "Your mama and y'all ain't nothing like my generation. We had to have a much thicker skin.

Couldn't just let everything going on in the world affect us like that." Nana blows smoke above my head and stares at me like she's waiting for me for me to say something back. I'm trying to rearrange what she's said in my mind to not mean that she thinks my mama was weak. That my mama cared too much about everything for her to be strong enough to survive being alive.

———

"I'm not finna do that, Yaminah."

"Why not, because I'm a girl?"

"No. Because I know you don't really want to do it. You just goin' through some shit right now. You gon' regret it in the morning." Maleek's cut off the clippers while Kobe sits in the barber chair waiting for us to stop arguing. He runs his fingers through the front of his locs and stares at me for a second before turning his attention back to the surgical operation that is his brother's head.

"How you know what I'ma regret in the morning?"

"I just know. You ain't never wanted to do nothing like this before and ain't no comin' back from that. At least not for a few years," he says, gliding his clippers upward on the side and behind Kobe's ear while he holds it. I don't like the way he's already broken eye contact with me as if whatever he says is final. I don't like that he doesn't believe me when I tell him what I want to do. And I definitely don't like that he keeps acting like he knows me better than I know myself after all these years. Kobe goes back to scrolling in his phone as thick tufts of his hair fall around him onto the floor. For a moment I listen closer to the whir of clothes wrestling inside the dryer on the other side of the wall that separates us from the laundry room.

Maleek's got all his tools laid out on a long shelf attached under a large, smudged mirror. There's one smaller set of clippers, oil sheen spray, a razor blade, scissors, and a comb on top of towel. On one side of the mirror there's a vintage poster of different haircuts posed at a variety of angles, numbered one through twenty-five, by a bunch of black boys who'd gotten their hair cut expertly. Kobe and Maleek could have been any one of those black boys back when we were kids scooting around in church pews wearing stuffy suits and itchy lace dresses, waiting for the three- and four-hour services to end. Using the hand that's not cutting Kobe's hair, Maleek brushes his brother's scalp gently every few minutes with laser focus as he moves across his head in a trancelike rhythm. His phone buzzes on the shelf and he pauses to check the name that flashes across the screen. I grab the clippers out of his hand.

TWENTY-TWO

Tiff shows me around downtown Obsidian like a guide leading a sheltered tourist to the light.

And there are lights everywhere you look. Obsidian, Michigan, isn't exactly the type of city anybody would normally think of for vacation or a reckless weekend out with the homies like Las Vegas or Cancun, but it's obvious that it wants to be. From the tapas bars—what Tiff calls these fancy-ass restaurants where white fraternity bros pay way too much money for crumbs—to the new skyscraping luxury lofts, to the decked-out concert venues featuring artists that never would have coughed in our direction before, the OB is being taken over. Inch by inch every vacant lot, open field, or deserted neighborhood looking delicious to businessmen pressed to abbreviate our neighborhoods into something up and coming. Clearly, they couldn't care less about how things were before. Not gonna lie, though. It sure looks pretty. Pretty as hell.

"Yo, why you talkin' to me like I ain't never been downtown before?"

"Well, because technically you haven't been. Anything before high school don't count. Plus everything *is* different. Besides . . . you came walkin' out Nana's looking like a new bitch so I'm treating you like one," she smirks, pausing in the center of the newly paved fashion-district pathway. I graze my head, suddenly feeling the coolness of my fingers against scalp, naked for the first time. Maleek had no choice after I drove the clippers down the center of my head. Him and Kobe might fight each other out on the front lawn sometimes but nobody in that house was about to let me walk out the door looking like nobody cared about me. Nana shook her head at me like I was a lost cause the second she saw me step through the basement door, but she looked down into her hands and told me I reminded her of her baby. Bold as I wanna be just like my mama, she said.

"Come on, let's stop in here." We duck into a place called Taco Flacko that Tiff later tells me is a Mexican dive bar where, in just a few steps, we're underground beneath twinkling blue lights. The ceiling makes me feel a lot taller than I am, low and lined with Christmas lights, and in the back is a pool table surrounded by vintage arcade games. I don't really listen to what Tiff's telling me, talking all animated with her hands, distracted by the college-aged dudes hovering over the green felted table. All of them briefly peer at us over their bottles. I can't believe I'm in here and, for a second, worry that somebody who could tell stories of when I used to be in diapers might see me. Hometown problems. I can't even imagine what Pop would do if he caught us. But he's not here right now and Tiff tells me she knows the bartender, so we sit at a small table close enough for her to order us drinks without drawing too much attention.

"These your new people?" I ask Tiff as the bartender lowers two drinks in plastic soda cups onto the table. She lingers for half a second and winks at Tiff before going back to her post.

"Whatchu mean, 'my new people'? They know me, I know them. They know I work crazy hours over at the stadium and we look out for each other. They don't make me pay for nothin' or card my friends, and I let them cut the line or get them into the shows for free. Plus working these events and in bars around here gets a little wild sometimes," she says, pausing to take a sip of her drink. "We're sort of like a little family. You want a taste of this?" She pushes her drink into my hands before I even have a chance to respond.

"Damn, this actually tastes good. It's prolly weak, though."

"What you know about a weak drink? You're barely sixteen." Now Tiff sounds like Pop even though she's only a few years over sixteen herself. I feel the press of the crowd get a little closer as the voices and music surrounding us raises with it. I gulp down Tiff's drink. "What the fuck, Minah?" She sounds annoyed but she's got this weird smirk on her face that tells me she's not mad for real and that she can order another.

"These are free, right?"

"Yeah, but chill. Take it easy." She signals to the bartender while I gulp down my Long Island iced tea, a drink I'd heard the name of in a movie somewhere, and I'm surprised that there's no burn. No nasty aftertaste and I'm convinced that, even though they're letting us drink, they're treating me like a child. I ask her to order me two. She pauses for a minute, looking at me as if I don't understand what I'm asking or like maybe she doesn't know me as well as she thought. I do understand, and neither do I. Five minutes later, two fully tatted arms drop off three more drinks along with tacos, waffle fries, and some rainbow-colored dessert thing that I don't remember Tiff ordering.

Behind our table, a line of girls with long, stringy blond hair and maybe one black guy who looks like he works on computers all day starts growing. So does the sloppiness of everyone around us. Between the multiple screens above the bar showing a live MMA fight, about three screens with red numbers of upcoming orders, and the constant *ding* of the games being played in the backroom just a few feet away, everything swarming around in my mind begins to grow louder while our immediate surroundings blend into a thick, sweaty blur. All of a sudden, each thing I touch is too damp to grasp and the ground beneath me is so wavy, I'm ready to go for a swim.

———————

There was a second box I found under my mama's bed. Another shoebox but unmarked and much harder to pull out into the open. This one was filled with diaries.

I didn't know Sandra wrote things down. I knew she kept cards, letters, and invitations people gave her even before I found the first box but I never saw her with a pen scribbling into some private notebook that she didn't want us to see. These must be from other times. Times that we didn't know her and she was just a girl and, later, a woman who belonged to nobody. Not even her own kids. It seemed like Sandra said everything that was on her mind the minute her mouth felt like it. The way her voice would take up a whole room was like nobody else. And it made sense. Ever since me and Fati could understand full words she'd tell us about her life before us. How she never meant to become a nurse; our mama was going to be a performer like Whitney Houston or Jenifer Lewis. She could hold any note and lift her leg straight up to the ceiling in a split ever since she was our age, she'd said. Sandra always told us she could do it all and that's why she knew the both of us would be fine, no matter what happened to her. I could never think of what could happen to our mama at the time. To me, mamas and daddies lived forever even if we did see Nana getting old. Nobody could tell me our parents would ever get old like Granny.

But Mama always had a special look in her eye. Like wasn't no way life as it was could ever be enough for her. At first, it looked like the sparkle someone gets when they dream of things that nobody in their life's ever been able to do. The one that lets everybody know there's nothing about to get in their way. Then, that sparkle turned into a lifeless glint, like something reflected off a mirage in a scene on television. Sandra's sparkle became nothing but a performance, us always crossing our fingers for a chance to go to her show. One of the last times me and Fati watched a movie with her was at Nana's house. A few days after Sandra had moved back in with Nana but was still pretending things would be all good. That things would go back to normal again one day soon. We were all piled up in the TV room on Nana's old tweed couch. Nana's couch stunk but we just liked being able to braid the strings while Mama held us in her arms, one of her girls on each side. Her favorites were the black-and-white movies, more than anything else. That night Fati asked her why. Unlike our old toy chest filled with black Barbies, these old movies were so white and we didn't know anybody that lived like the actors. Mama just smiled her tired smile and said, "The white folks just look so happy and when I'm watchin' them be happy, I'm happy, too."

It seemed a little strange to me back then how watching people that don't look anything like us live perfect lives could ever make somebody like Sandra happy, too. But that answer was good enough. Mama was smiling and that's the part we never wanted to end. I lift all three of Sandra's diaries out of the box and brush off the dust. Along the spine, each of them were marked by year. I could tell by the covers and the handwriting which ones were from when she was much younger. I cracked open the one from 2017.

November 3, 2017

Mama is tellin' everybody I'm sick. That I got cancer. Guess that's much easier than telling them there's something I love more than

anything else. More than her. And that there's no money left, living in
her house like I ain't a grown-ass woman. I just needed something for
the pain. I just needed everything to slow down, stop. This life is such
a never-ending nightmare and nobody tells you how to deal while
you really going through it. They just tell you to pray. They tell you to
stop crying. Stop being so sad. Stop being such a Debbie Downer all
the time and then judge you when you find something that makes you
happy. Something that makes you forget about it all. Nobody told me
being somebody's mama would be like two hands wrapped around my
throat, squeezing. Harder and harder. Knowing when they don't have
something, need something, everybody looks at you. Somebody's hand is
always out, looking at me. Wanting me to be around. But I don't even
want me around. I need the world to stop wanting me. Wanting. I wish
it would just all stop.

I don't know where I'm going but I know I have to go. Now. I can barely
focus on one Tiffany, let alone the three of her sitting next to me asking if I'm okay. Telling me maybe I need to slow down. Looking at me
like we need to go home. I settle for a glance in her direction and then
I'm stumbling toward the door. I think she calls me a few times as I
swim through a crowd of people reeking of alcohol on the way out. A
dude I've never seen before tries to grab my hand. "Who the FUCK are
YOU?" is all I manage to fling his way, fighting to steady my legs so he
doesn't think it'd be easy to take me home. My back is already turned
to him before I can even think about seeing what he wants. I feel a
growing heat swarm around me just as Tiff makes it outside but I can't
wait for her.

"Minah, hold up!" she calls behind me. "Minah, wait! Where are you even going?" No words come to me. She won't understand and I feel too tired to even try so I'm walking far away from Taco Flacko. I hear Tiff's feet trailing behind, trying to catch up, and no matter how hard I try to slow down, my legs won't listen. Is it still where it was when we were kids? Is it possible to gentrify a cemetery? "Minah, stop! The car isn't even this way. What are you doing?" I try to tell her that I'm going for a walk and, instead, I hear myself make gibberish words toward the sky. My body starts to grow heavy and I think to lie down right there on the sidewalk, but then I see the sign just a half block up, just past the stoplight:

LOWER OBSIDIAN MEMORIAL GROUND.

The day it all gets to be too much, it feels like the only thing you can do is run. Run fast, far away from here until you lose all of your breath. From the very first day that you're born you're already dying anyway. But just as soon as you learn words, everybody around you is using them to lie. To pretend that it'll all be okay. That the pain will end. That there will be an explanation for everything if you're patient. If you just wait and see. They won't even talk about it. The only thing for sure is your life will end and it's because your body has had enough. You have had enough trying. Trying to be alive is a lot of work all by itself, but then people come around and make it even harder. Ask you for things. Tell you things that don't make sense and leave you to figure out the truth by yourself. Nobody tells you that no matter how many people you are around, you are always alone. There is nobody in the world that can be with you one hundred percent of the time. You are the only person with you one hundred percent of the time. So even though it don't make sense, you listen when something tells you to run. Run past all the buildings. Run past every car, every stoplight. Run past the sign and hop the fence. Run past all the other stones with bodies buried in the ground. Run until you find the name. Find the name that matches yours. Find me. Run even though you're slipping. Run even though you're falling. Run until your breath has nowhere else to guide you but back to where it first started to hurt.

TWENTY-THREE

"You gonna keep starin' at me like that or are you gon' get in? Come on now! The water'll get cold if you don't hurry up. I'm sure you wanna get out of those nasty clothes! You smell like peanut butter, baby, and not in a good way."

Sandra sits at the edge of the tub with her house shoes kicked off, testing the water, and flicking the suds off her fingers while I pull my T-shirt up over my head, then slip out of my jeans. "I put the lemon bubble bath you like in there too, girl, come on. It's been a long night. I'm not mad at you, baby." I expect the open air to be cold once all of my clothes are on the floor but the bathroom is oddly warm as if it's the exact temperature of my body. Sandra stretches her hand out toward me as I step in, using the other hand to steady myself on the tub's edge, one foot at a time. "There you go. Go'on and sink all the way in. Don't worry about that hair. You know your granny tore my ass up the first time I got to' up."

"How old were you, Mama?"

"I think I was around your age. Mm-hmm . . . Fast tail out in these streets, okay?!" It's hard to imagine my mama doing things us teenagers do and, later, getting in trouble with Nana. Her and Pop joked sometimes about her sneaking out to see him or him climbing into her window when Nana was asleep, but it felt a little too weird thinking about her at parties sweaty and pushed up against a wall or sitting on any boy's lap when she was in high school. I know what high school boys are like, and envisioning my mama dealing with it is just a little too much. She lifts one of my arms and glides the soapy sponge across it after dunking it into the water. She blows a lump of bubbles off her arm into my face and I catch the hint of grape soda on her breath. Her favorite flavor. "Ain't nothin' new under the sun, baby. I know what it's like to wanna escape."

I sink deeper into the tub until the water's just below my earlobes. Mama's eyes make me feel like a specimen under a microscope, wiggling around beneath a bright light being examined all the way down to my nose hairs. She dunks the sponge again and brings it to my neck to wash my collarbone. I shiver under her touch, trying hard not to laugh even though she knows how ticklish I am. She goes to lift my other arm to scrub my armpit and I cave. She stops and leans back.

"Laugh, child!" she screams, giving me full permission.

Snot comes flying out of my noise almost immediately with her permission to let out all that I'd been holding in. We're both laughing so hard we have to grab our aching bellies. The bathtub is the perfect place to accidentally cry. "I'm sorry, Mama. I didn't mean to . . . I was just . . ."

"Shh . . . ain't nothin' wrong with tears. Shit, you already in the tub. Ain't no better place, if you ask me."

"It's just . . . I just miss you so much."

"Well, I'm right here, baby. I'm right here." She's right here.

"Mama?"

"Yeah, baby?" She puts one hand on the back of my neck and I know to let my head fall all the way back. A small plastic container filled with water appears in her other hand and she pours this over my head, letting it fall through my hair and down my back. She immediately does this again.

"What's your favorite color?"

"Now, how you gon' ask me that? You know what my favorite color is."

"I mean . . . I know you like to wear purple but I don't mean that."

"Well then, what you mean, baby?" A large white shampoo bottle appears in her hand and she pours out enough purple shampoo to fill her entire hand.

"Like, what's your favorite color to look at?"

She chuckles to herself like she's been waiting for me to ask this for a long time, but like she knew this was the exact moment when it would come up. She leans forward and starts to scrub my scalp.

"Well, that's easy, baby. Red. Every time I look at it, I think about what it might feel like to be powerful." Her nails dig into the top of my head and then she moves to the sides before standing up to scrub the back. My neck starts to ache a little but I don't tell her.

"Why don't you ever wear it, then?" The light falls out of her eyes.

"Guess I just felt like it wasn't ever the color for me. It don't feel like power is something your mama ever really had. Powerful ain't something I could ever be. Lay back." The way Mama tells me to lay down makes me feel like I don't have a choice. Like if I don't do it as fast as I can, I won't like the way she makes me. I scoot my butt farther down the tub to make enough room for me to drop my hair all the way into the water. Like soap suds, Mama's words swarm around in my head while she pours the cup over my head again and again. On the fourth or fifth pour, I notice she isn't stopping. "I'm gon' throw those clothes of yours in the washer right after this. Smells like you really had a night just like your mama used to do."

"I think all the shampoo's out now, Mama."

"Who's washing your hair? You or me?"

"I just . . . I can feel it—"

"I did my best, you know. It's just that when me and your pop got married, everything started happening so fast. Nobody understands." She dipped the cup in the tub again, and this time when it passes over-head, I see the water is red. "And we were young. So young. Were we just supposed to stop having a life? I mean, your daddy was okay with stayin' at home, gettin' old, and that being it. But me? That shit started feeling like I couldn't breathe."

"Mama—"

"I didn't know I would like it that much and it ain't seem like that much of a big deal, okay? I just needed something to take the edge off. So much pressure." She pauses with a handful of my hair in her hand to stare off into space. "If I knew it was gon' ruin my whole life, I would have never tried it. I would have said no, baby, I swear! And I look at you. I see you takin' walks around the block the way I used to do." She emphasizes the word *walks*, aware that I know what that really means, and chuckles, shaking her head to herself. "I see the way you've shaved that head of yours thinking it's gon' change something, gon' make your mind feel less cloudy. I hear the way you talk to your daddy and the way you get all riled up sometimes when it all gets to be too much and I can see myself, baby." The whole tub has turned red, all of the water engulfing me, thick like paint, and now there's too much of it everywhere. I try to sit up to get closer to her. To reach for her hand, her arm, something. I need to turn the water back on, unplug the drain, and rinse whatever this is off me; but she lets go of my hair and places her hand on my chest. "Be honest: It feels good, doesn't it? The way your lips get numb and the way your body starts floating. Your legs becoming like Jell-O, nothing standing in your way. No inhibitions. You act like I was such a terrible mother. Like I was so bad you could leave me behind for good. But look at you, following in my footsteps. Look at you just trying to escape, too."

"No disrespect, Mama. But I don't want to be like you." She laughs, tobacco smoke huffing from her mouth. The tub's tide rises until the water runs over the edge and spills onto the floor, flooding Mama's feet, my clothes, in between every corner and crease of the bathroom. I reach for the tub's edge again, trying to pull myself up, but the water is too heavy. I take a deep breath the way somebody winces before being punched.

"Well, that's too damn bad, baby. 'Cause you already are." The air is too heavy and Mama is just watching me drown. She laughs again.

"No, I'm not! I could never become like you," I growl, smoke racing out of my mouth as I feel myself sink deeper. My head finally falls all the way under and I hear her laugh even harder, her voice muffled beyond the water.

"Oh yeah?" Through the layer of red above me, I see her blurry figure stand up to walk away to where I can only hear her from a distance.

Then swim.

TWENTY-FOUR

"Ain't you too old to still be having night terrors?"

"What you mean, ain't I too old? You the same age as me."

"Correction," Fati says, raising her pointer finger in front of my face. "I'm seven minutes and thirteen seconds older than you. Put some respect on your big sister's name. Especially since I came all the way up here to take care of your sloppy ass." Hoisting myself up halfway on my elbows, I look around Sandra's room, apparently the site of a tornado that's just passed through. Fati is sitting by my side, leaned against the headboard like she's been there for hours waiting for me to come back to life.

"What the hell is that smell?"

"You, Minah. It's you. You're lucky I didn't make you sleep in those clothes, either. Guess it pays to be your twin after all. Changing you out of those puke-stained clothes was just like undressing myself. Kobe carried you up here, though. Wasn't no way me or Tiff could have got you up two whole flights of stairs." She gently dabs the sweat pooled on my forehead with a damp towel and I rest back onto the pillow. With the other hand she grazes my head with her full hand, like she's assessing a different version of herself in the mirror. "Well, almost like undressing myself. You different for real now," she says, pausing as if she's taking that idea in before standing up and handing me the towel. "Here, take it. I'm not about to bathe you, sis. My shift is over."

"Wait." She stops at the door and turns around, her eyes glancing over the room.

"Yeah?"

"Thanks for taking care of me."

"It's all good. I mean . . . it ain't *all* good. We got a lot to talk about, but I wasn't gon' leave you hangin' like you did me. We family," she says, looking down at her fingers. I deserved all of that. "I . . . I still think about her a lot, too. You aren't the only one who she comes to visit in dreams, neither." Fati bends down. She picks up my T-shirt and jeans, then closes the door behind her.

———

"All right now, go'on 'head and squeeze in. C'mon now, closer. Yes, even closer. Damn, can y'all just act like you love each other for five seconds?"

Fati might be talking to me again but Pop is doing way too much. Us talking isn't enough for him; to seal the deal we gotta be all mushy and touch elbows on some *Brady Bunch* shit. "Yo, can you just take the picture? I'm hot and Robyn ain't finna stay in my hands too much longer. She don't like the spotlight, like her mama," Fati says, shifting her weight and scooting Robyn higher up on her hip. Pop tries several different poses before he's satisfied with the pictures. Not us, him. First, he tries standing super far back because he claimed he needed to get the view of the Obsidian River behind us. Then, he had to try super up close because he said he needed to be able to see the "joy of reuniting" on us.

"Reunited and it feeeeels so gooood," he sang back to our scrunched faces. Then he had to try one last time laying in the grass on his side like he said he's seen real photographers do to get the "money shot."

Fati and I decide the photo shoot's over after that one and collapse under a tree by the water. "All right, all right. Can't blame your old man for trying." He pulls a large blanket out of his gym bag and spreads it out for us all to move onto. Robyn squirms out of Fatimah's hands and jumps into Pop's just as he sets out some of the food.

"Paw Paw," she says, looking up into his eyes expectantly, with a two-year-old's face Pop has seen twice before when he was fourteen years younger. Pop's only known he's a grandfather for a few days now and he's already a natural baby magnet. For a second a look of guilt washes over his eyes but he blinks it away just as quickly as it comes. I mean, all the time lost isn't exactly his fault. Pop called and called for a long time. Fatimah just stopped picking up.

"And you said she takes a lot of time to get warmed up. Look at her. Already in love with me."

"She just knows you're the one with all the food," Fati cuts with a smirk.

"Yeah, yeah, say what you want. She loves me 'cause I'm Paw Paw."

"Chuice, Paw Paw? Wahmella?"

"See, my baby gets right to the point. She knows how to ask for what she needs." Pop opens the container of watermelon, plunging a plastic fork into the first piece Robyn points to. Doing his best airplane impression, he dodges Robyn's mouth, zooming the fruit around her head, up high and low until she pouts, telling him, "Gimme peez. Gimme!"

"All right, all right," he says, giving her the piece of fruit. "Since your cute self asked so nicely. My grandbaby got all the manners. Who taught you that?"

"Mommy," she says.

"Oh yeah?" Pop asks, looking at both of us as Robyn nods her head.

"More peez." This is when the sound of the maple tree leaves crashing against each other above us takes over. Then the gentle rush of river water over rocks that me and Fati used to hop between, holding hands so we didn't fall in. Robyn's watermelon chewing slices through it all and we turn our focus onto to her, the easiest distraction from the fact that we're here. Together. Without Mama. Pop scratches his head, trying on different ways of sitting, the way he tried different angles to capture his two daughters on camera after all these years.

"Is it so bad?" Fati begins, turning her attention to Pop. "Is it so bad being here?" Pop scratches the back of his head, looking down for a moment. Then he looks out onto the river and across the park before taking a few deep breaths like he's trying to find the courage to tell Fati the truth.

"It never really was, Crunch," he says back, addressing her by his nickname for her for the first time in years, and it sounds strange coming out of his mouth. Almost like he lost the right to call her anything but her first name years ago. I feel Fati cringe a little bit under his quiet plea to know her by nickname again. "But change is good. We needed a change." I sit between them, hoping Pop has more to say than that. Fati deserves a lot more. "But I know that don't make none of it feel any better. I should have been there for both of you. I was tryna give us a fresh start after things ain't work out for me and your mama, but I couldn't even get you to pack a suitcase. I didn't want y'all to see any more fighting so I let you and your mama win. But I'd made my mind up about having to leave to help us move on and maybe I could have found a better way."

"I'm glad I stayed, Pop," Fati continues. "At least now Robyn gets to grow up around family. And maybe one day she'll get to grow up in a house where she has her own room. And now that Minah's bald-headed, I won't have to worry about Robyn getting confused when y'all visit," she says, briefly glancing over at me with a slight smirk. "Besides," Fati continues, "I couldn't leave Mama. Sometimes it felt like I was all she had. Or at least the only one who understood her." It's Fati's turn to look off into the distance, now. Part of me feels like she misses us and the other part of me feels like it's too late. Hearing her talk about Robyn growing up here bulldozes through any hopes I'd started to develop about her coming back to Brooklyn with me. It was a selfish idea that I'd just thought up, not thinking about the life she already has here, anyway. Pop suddenly starts rummaging through his gym bag, then stops and snaps his fingers, pulling his wallet out of his back pocket like that's where he should have started in the first place. Robyn wobbles back over to Fati and collapses between her legs, drinking from her sippy cup like she's just run miles. There's probably nothing that could replace Mama's lap.

"I got something I want y'all to see," Pop says, opening his wallet. He scoots closer to the both of us, extending a picture that he's pulled from it, and we all stare at it for a very long time. In the center a man that looks too familiar stands with his arms behind Sandra's and Pop's backs. He's only a little taller than Sandra, wearing a Kangol hat, a short-sleeve flannel shirt that's tucked into some of the most embarrassing-looking jeans I've ever seen. He looks like he's got salt all over his beard and mustache. But his smile, though a little tooth deficient, is so big I smile back accidentally. At the bottom of the picture, small orange digital-looking numbers read OCT 9 2000. I'm confused.

"Is that your dad?" Fati asks. We've never seen any pictures of Pop's parents. All we ever knew is that they passed before we were old enough to meet them and since we aren't in the picture, it would make sense. But I can't shake the feeling that I've seen him somewhere before.

"That's Benny. He's your grandpop. He's your mama's daddy."

Benny. BENNY. And the same way it happens in the movies, my brain flashes back to the day Nana told us she was selling the house as he was kept in the back, eating off a plate Uncle James made for him. My whole body gets sad at whatever this means before I can even fully figure it out.

"I saw him the other day," I blurt out. "Well, a lot of us saw him the other day."

"I figured you might, Munch," he says, scratching the back of his head again.

"And I see him all the time," Fati adds.

"But it doesn't make any sense. How could *he* be our grandfather if he wasn't even invited to the family reunion? And why did he look like that? *Smell* like that?" I'm feeling all kinds of chaos at once. Grandfathers are supposed to be there when you visit for the holidays. Sneak you extra candy when your parents aren't looking. Slip five-dollar bills into your hands when they get news from the tooth fairy that you lost another one. Sit at the best table at the BBQs, playing dominos with their elderly friends.

Grandfathers aren't supposed to be wandering the streets alone. Sleeping on empty park benches. Arriving at family gatherings hoping for scraps. Begging strangers who are actually their granddaughters for loose change. I think about avoiding Old Man and buying him coffee when he recognizes me on the way to buy snacks from Bobby. Maybe his grandkids feel the same way I feel right now . . . if he has any. My body's temperature starts climbing as Fati's hand moves to my lower back. She tells me to take a breath. "What happened to him, Pop?"

Robyn crawls over to the corner of the blanket where Pop's left an open bag of sour cream and onion chips. She looks over her shoulder back to her mother as if to ask if it's okay and Fati nods, her eyes welled up like a levee before it breaks. I reach for her hand.

"Y'all's mama was just like her pop, Munch. Sensitive. Caring. One of the biggest hearts god ever put in a person. But the world don't always look out for the ones who give the most. Sometimes all the world does is take. And that's what happened to him. He lost a lot of things in his lifetime, including his last job over in Onyx Hill where all the black businesses used to be after all the new construction projects started. Well, I-479, now," he adds, shaking his head. "He ain't never get back on his feet after that. And you know . . . people like your grand-pop and your mama get down on theyself when the pressure gets to be too much." Pop pauses and takes a deep breath, grazing his head and then clutching his right arm with his left. He looks up, his eyes welling, darting back and forth between me and Fati's. "I think y'all are old enough now to understand that if you do certain things too much they become a problem. In your mama's case, it ain't take her trying it more than once. Your mama loved you both so much. Just like I know your grandpop still does. And she would still be here, loving you, if she hadn't developed a disease."

"Mommy, why chucrine?" All of us are crying as Robyn attempts to wipe her mother's eyes, probably thinking mommies aren't ever supposed to fall apart this way. "Issokay, Mommy. Issokay," she continues to say, squirming her way back into Fatimah's lap, wrapping her small arms around her sides.

"Addiction is a disease that the world has very little compassion for. I was upset at your mama for a long time. For getting involved in that mess. For not telling me what was going on inside of her. She didn't know what it was when she tried it, and by the time we realized, the woman I knew was long gone. I was angry that she let this happen to us but now I know she couldn't help it much and that it wasn't about me. She wasn't happy and it took me too long to see it. For everybody to see it." Fati squeezes my hand as I squeeze hers, Pop's words burning my ears even though him telling us all of this is overdue. "But I'm paying attention now. And I love the both of you. And if you ever feeling like everything is too much, I don't want you to be too scared to tell somebody. This world don't make it easy to ask for help, but your pain won't bother me."

"Only thing scared around here is that hairline running away from your *face!*" Fati says under her breath, wiping her eyes with a cheesy grin on her face. I snort and we all bust out laughing, grateful for a brief change in subject. Pop pretends to be offended and throws on his baseball cap.

"Ain't nobody scared, huh?" Pop taunts, standing up to dust off his pants. He walks away and stops at the tree where our races always used to start. "Put your money where your mouth is, Crunch. You and me. Whoever loses has to treat the winner to ice cream when we leave." And Fati plays the card that Pop owes her for ever leaving her behind. She doesn't get up, she just stares back, arms wrapped around Robyn. "All right, I hear you," he says, walking back over to us. "Double-scoop waffle cones on me."

My babies. I hope now you can see me for who I really was. Somebody who ain't always know how to be your mama. Somebody who ain't know how to be. Just a person. I did my best, though. Loved you from the only love I ever knew. But sometimes that love hurt me on the inside. Sometimes it hurt too much. You needing me and me not even being enough for myself. For your pop. I was just starting to live and here you two come needing little old me. I asked god how I was s'posed to do this and he ain't really say nothin' back. I mean everybody thought we was doing great and we was, but then I thought about the rest of our lives and it just hurt a lot. Y'all bein' so perfect when I'm not. I want y'all to know that I love you, still. And every day I watch you hopin' you find the things I left for you. Pieces of me so you can piece it all together. The stuff you been needing to know from your mama even though she ain't here. I left you my love, if you'll believe it. A love so big it broke my heart in two and I spent all those years tryna feel something good again. Something bigger than bein' afraid. Something bigger than the voices telling me I was gon' mess this up. Mess you up. I know they think I ain't hear it when they warned y'all about me. About how y'all shouldn't ever be like me. But who was gon' tell you how I got to be like this? Who was gon' tell the truth about how I was down to try anything to escape this dusty earth? Even if it meant leaving my babies. My babies. Won't nobody know exactly how you feel so I hope you get to know exactly how you feel, if nothing else. Listen when you ache. Cry if you feel something needs to come out. Say yes to nothing you ain't ready for and don't nobody tell you when you ready. Don't let nobody ever tell you need to be ready. Your mama loves you but I wasn't ready. I don't know if I was ever meant to be. But y'all are the best surprise I ever made 'cause you get to make something different.

I know we ain't talk too much after a while. I know I went away, and you couldn't reach me. But think about me sometimes, will you? Think about the good times.

I know it wasn't all bad. You and me, we used to smile.

EPILOGUE

A rumor about Obsidian, Michigan, goes like this:

There once were two boys who took things. But not in the way that people might think. The things the boys were taking weren't small things like candy or beer from the store on the corner, no. They weren't taking food or their grandmother's last nerve. The two boys took bigger things that they said never belonged to their new owners in the first place. According to the neighborhood, it was impossible, though. Because these two boys weren't about anything—no college, no regular jobs—and where were they getting house-type money? First, the rumor was that they were doing things in alleyways after dark that they had no business doing. That the money was no good to their grandmother. The rumor was that, at first, they blew it all the way young boys do when they see that kind of cash. But that wasn't true. These boys knew what they wanted to do with their money. They knew why they had to start taking. They knew they had to find a way to stay.

So the boys carried on. Doing god knows what with god knows who, and the money began to stack higher than they've ever seen. Than anyone in their family had ever seen. They did this until there was enough to be taken serious. Enough to quiet the thieves. The thieves with real estate licenses and notebooks and cameras. They became smarter than the thieves and began to play the game, too. But backward.

First for their grandmother's house. Then their cousins', the two girls. Piecing together a family. Figuring out where the baby would live. What they were doing was inevitable, really. The taking and no longer asking. The breaking-in. The heist of everything that was stolen from them. The stolen blocks becoming theirs again. It was owed.

The rumor spread, and the boys stopped being the only ones taking things back. The rumor spread further than this small corner of Obsidian. Soon it permeated the whole state. Then the country.

It was chaos at first.

But only at first.

Acknowledgments

This book came to me in a dream over five years ago and turned into something completely different by the time it was fully written. I barely recognize it. I want to thank my editor, Andrew Karre, for encouraging the chaos and trusting my vision. Thank you for not standing in the way the many times I changed my mind.

I also want to thank me. Because writing this book was one of the most painful things I've ever done and I'm proud of me for not quitting when it got rough. I can look back now and say it was all worth it.

And to my friends and close creative community: thank you for holding space for all my grief.